BUILD
UNIVERSES

Patricia Walsh

In The Days
of Ford Cortina

Patricia
Walsh

europe books

© 2021 **Europe Books** | London
www.europebooks.co.uk – info@europebooks.co.uk

ISBN 979-12-201-1014-3
First edition: June 2021

Distribution for the United Kingdom: **Vine House Distribution ltd**

Printed for Italy by Rotomail Italia
Finito di stampare nel mese di giugno 2021
presso Rotomail Italia S.p.A. - Vignate (MI)

In The Days of Ford Cortina

In memory of my father
Thomas
(1932 - 2009)
And my mother
Teresa
(née Cunnane)
(1938 - 2011)

Special thanks goes to Mel O'Dea for meticulously going through the various drafts of this novel.

To Paul Casey and my compatriots at the Ó Bhéal poetry night in Cork city, for giving me an avenue on which to cut my literary teeth. Regards to Charles Clarke and Rab Urquhart for making sure I was well rested and fed these past few years.

To my best friend from school, Siobhán Byrne, for putting up with so much for so long, and to my flatmate and close friend Justin Kelleher, for the same reason.

To my siblings, Claire, Deirdre, Declan, and Carmel, and my various nieces and nephews, for making the ride worthwhile.

CHAPTER 1

- Slam the door behind you, if you wish, said Sr Eucharia.

For once, Cortina did as she was told. The slam sent shockwaves through the corridor and spilt, as she sensed, out into the teachers' car park. She stayed outside momentarily, enough to listen to the nuggets of wisdom from the teachers that was almost down to a cliché regarding her situation.

- Did you see how readily she took that expulsion order – no whimpering, no explanation, excuse, nothing! It's almost insulting! And for what? Over stealing a DVD player! snarled Ms Clarke, the vice-principal.

- That was just a technicality; she was heading that way anyway, intoned Ms Parlin, the class teacher.

- You have to feel sorry for her; she never had a mother to set her straight. She died young, to the best of my recollection. Poor thing, said Eucharia.

- Thought Marie, you know, Ms. Masterson, the new teacher, would have sorted her out, being engaged to her dad and all that, but she's actually gotten worse, if that were possible. Ms Clarke said with a resigned air.

- I understand her home life is far from happy. Can't really blame her for going the way she did. Never had a mother to look after her, her father at a loss to control her, let her away with too much for too long. Maybe Marie Masterson would set her straight, after all. You can have all the bog psychology you want but it doesn't take from the fact that Cortina is just plain nuts, and insolent at that. Couldn't call it unexpected, to paraphrase Elvis Costello, said Eucharia.

- She's maladjusted if that's a criterion anymore, quipped Ms. Parlin.

- She didn't fit the autism spectrum, said Sr Eucharia, she's just very badly behaved, if such a thing existed anymore, that doesn't have a fancy name attached to it. She had her final warning a few weeks back when she threw all the water in the gym toilets, said Eucharia.

- She's superstitious, she won't work on any day with a 'y' in it. Said Ms. Clarke, trying to raise a laugh.

- She's a criminal in the making. Napoleon of crime as far as the school's concerned, sighed Eucharia.

- She's lucky she has friends in high places, Marie had to talk Garda Dunne out of making an arrest.

- There's hope for her yet. As they say, young devil, old saint, like St Francis or the Buddha, said Ms. Parlin.

- But she's as cheeky...! We reprimanded her for smoking behind the gym often enough, she put up a fight there, even though we were smelling it off her clothes. Declared Ms. Clarke.

- She has the potential to be a straight A student but was not willing. Her house is left to her desolate. As we said, we thought Marie would sort her out, but she's having none of it, said Sr. Eucharia.

- Let's hope for the sake of everyone that it is just a phase she's going through, said Ms. Parlin.

- She's still outside the door, Sister. Tell her to get off the school grounds sharpish, said Ms. Clarke.

- Do you know about the water fight in the gym before the summer exams, supplying the water balloons that were thrown at the boys' academy – got them online? surmised Ms. Parlin.

- Was she suspended back then? inquired Ms. Clarke.

- That was her initial final warning, said Eucharia.

- Did you see her report cards? 'Has the ability, no effort' 'Constantly disruptive', I had to send her father a lengthy letter in addition to her report card - either improve grades or don't come back to this school. - First-rate brain, below average results, said Ms. Clarke.

- We were once told that you cannot divide by zero. She made a valiant attempt to do that with her report card, as you said. Her father was exasperated at meeting with you to explain the dismal test results. Had to explain why she shouldn't repeat the year, said Ms. Parlin.

- That's what bugs me, she's not stupid, and in fact, she's highly intelligent. She never uses her brains. She never works, said Eucharia.

- I thought geeks will inherit the earth. Probably fits the bill, said Ms Clarke.

- I seriously wish… said her father at the latest PTA meeting, that he could rip that intelligence out of her and give it to someone who could do with it! said Eucharia.

- She's still outside, said Ms. Parlin.

Sr Eucharia came up behind Cortina. True to form, she was there.

- Oh, by the way, Cortina, we forgot to switch the intercom off while we were talking to you. Goodbye. We'll slam the door for you.

The bell rang conveniently for lunch, and Cortina knew that now she was in trouble again, and not for the last time. Everyone's eyes were pointing at her, affixing blame where intended. She knew it would happen someday... and she was almost ecstatic.

CHAPTER 2

Next was the clearing out of her locker, fashioned with a tiny, almost novelty padlock. She conscientiously ignored the eyes and mouths of the entire school as she tweaked her padlock with a twist of her key and books and things tumbled out.

She bent down to pick them up, and she could not help but notice Annie, Vera, and Carol looking her up and down, before attempting to strike up a diplomatic conversation, even if they were a little unsympathetic.

- My life's mission is complete. I take it, you heard the news?

- Yes, Cortina. Pretty unfortunate but not entirely unpredictable. You had it coming.

- A big bag of tricks, eh?

- No, just things I need to clear up before I go. Just call me Cortina Murray - Child of Destiny.

Everyone tittered.

- Everyone knows your destiny is the primate house of Fota wildlife park.

- All they said about me attention seeking, I just want people off my case.

- You have now.

- Well, I suppose no prophet is honoured in his own country. Seek my fortune elsewhere.

- See? 'Become what you are'. That's a golden rule.

- And here's me thinking that your grand passion in life was giving Ms. Masterson a Glasgow kiss. Can't say fairer than that.

- Those teachers are fucking psychotic anyway!

- In every child, so say the nuns, there is a potential criminal which must be nipped in the bud if they want to progress.

- I'm into something bigger than that, something bigger than myself.

- What? Well? What? called out Annie.

- Are you plotting to kill? asked Vera.

- Nah, not worth the effort, but I tell you, if I could get off with killing one person, it would be Ms. Masterson. You know that. What's so fascinating about my life anyway? I'm just a joker, after all, a right royal pain in the ass at times for people, I'm nothing special.
- Maybe this will be good for you, ultimately. You can be a free spirit as much as you want

after the exams, but just knuckle down for the next few months and you'll be fine. And so will the rest of us... The next few years will fly anyway, for you as much as anyone.

- Whatever happened to 'education through laughter'?

- Not our idea of laughter. Or education.

- Maybe I will go on some sort of pilgrimage, like the Camino, make a grand passion in life. God knows I'm not staying out here. Serve in heaven, reign in hell. That's about the size of it. Think of all the books I haven't read. Now I can get started on them, I have all the time in the world.

- It doesn't matter if you don't have qualifications. You need those to get ahead.

- All those retarded creatures creaming themselves over my success. You know what they will say, 'Marie brought this wild girl to heel'– patting Ms Masterson on the back and me on the head. Not on my watch, they're not. They want me to be the token success story so enamoured of teachers. Just so they could show off what wonderful teachers they are.

- You do look for the wrong kind of attention, though, in fairnesss, said Annie.
- The smell of drink didn't do us any favours, though, or being drunk throughout double

19

Geography class, remember? Quipped Vera.

- You would suck the antifreeze out of the car radiator if you had to if you had no vodka or cigarettes. We won't get started about your antics at the Cigarette Tree, Cortina. That spot has your name on it, said Carol.

- Thank you for that observation. I'll bear that in mind.

- What are you going to do now? Being hyperactive and all that? Maybe it's down to you eating too much chocolate or sweets for that matter. Whatever about smoking, they say sugar is the new tobacco.

- As is said, if you dance to every jig, you will soon be lame in both legs. Stuff the experts, I am going home.

- Well, this serves you right. Having your father going out with one of our teachers might just be what you need. Straighten you out a bit.

- I don't need straightening out! We were all right until she came here!

- In fairness, we want to work and that means no fooling about from now on. It's getting boring, like Tallulah Bankhead.
- What about Tallulah Bankhead?

- You told us yourself, she was a Hollywood star more famous for her outrageous antics than her films.

- Most people actually mature as they get older, but you refuse to.

- Survival is in my hardwiring, get used to it.

- You need a mother figure to straighten you out, steer you in the right direction.

- I need a mother, I need a mother. I am so sick of hearing that. Well, let me tell you that I have spent most of my life without a mother and I am doing quite alright, thank you. My father can operate quite well on his own, thanks. As they say, two's company, three's a crowd. Crowding in, on my personal space, is something I can do without.

- How is your father going to handle this? What about his feelings?

- He's a hardworking single parent. No, double parent, he does the work of two parents. If the poles were reversed, if I had no father, the nuns would never have let end of it. Social mongrelism, or something like that, like my mother being a whore. I was very lucky that I was baptised, would never have gotten past the front gates of the school.
- What are you going to do now? Most schools don't accept expelled pupils.

- Don't worry, I'll manage. If Jonathan Philbin Bowman could get by, so can I. He left school after his Inter Cert and he did all right in the end, as a journalist and celebrity. Am I going to be missed? Have a going away party for me, hmm?

- Everyone knows that your ambition in life is to give Miss Masterson a permanent nosebleed.

- I'm too kind-hearted for the pleasures of bullying. I suffered that enough times myself and was living in the proverbial glass house that prevented me from projecting makeshift missiles.

- Humour was your stock-in-trade, kept the wolves, the bullies from her door. At least we weren't bored.

- Whatever about you, Cortina, some of us might want to work. Some of us might want decent grades. It was fun a few years ago, but it's tiresome now. Don't expect us to subscribe to your childish nonsense anymore. We got to the stage that people were drawing the short straw as to who would sit beside you in class.

- Yeah, ouch.
- You don't progress, and that's fine, but the problem is that you don't allow others to

progress. That's almost criminal.

- Maybe a mother figure will be good for you.

- Gestapo figure? No, thanks. I am going to go somewhere, where no one can reach me, where no one can reach me ever again! Pray God to stop this torture!

- Some would think that you were on a permanent mission to wind people up. You're just not news anymore. Or even funny.

- As Mark Twain once said, 'I have never let my schooling interfere with my education.' There's a veritable Eiffel Tower of books in my bedroom, all begging to be read. I can read all the books I want now. Now I can rise, phoenix-like, from the flames of the dross I was regularly fed at school. As Morrissey and the Smiths once said, 'There's more to life than books, you know, but not much more.'

- You are a failure, Cortina. Remember that, next time you are at the dole office, that's if you are over 18.

- You were never funny after a while, there is the difference between laughing 'with' and 'at'. People are getting sick of you, just knuckle down and work for once.

Cortina breathed a sigh of resignation. She knew that she was toast, as far as whole school was concerned. Even if she wanted to, she couldn't make her way back. She collected her books with what grace she could and made her way towards the door.

- Goodbye to you lads, thanks for everything. I'll never forget you, she wistfully said, as anyone could do under the circumstances.

- What will you do now? Home schooling?

- Over my dead body, with *her*. Just have to assess the situation and take it from there.

- We have work to do, with or without you. You're holding us back. You're not so much the class clown as the school joke. That's why we all cheered when you got expelled, we heard it over the intercom. Everyone did, the whole school, in fact

It hurt her deeply but knew enough not to let it show in public. Anyway, what had she to worry about? As she cleaned out the remnants of her locker, she spotted a few library books tumbling out.

- Have to return these while I still remember. Here I keep my nose clean, even though I didn't up till now.

CHAPTER 3

She turned the corner very quickly into the library, not caring who would be in her path. The library was in a relatively new part of the school, so it didn't have that old book smell hitting you on the way in, like the library in town. Not to worry, there were always good books if you knew where to find them. She hoped against hope that Alison, the school librarian would be there. She was.

- I'm returning my books for the last time.

- Heard your news. Shame about you going like that! You were the only student in the whole school who reads anywhere on a regular basis.

- You were the only member of staff whom I could tolerate. All those teachers are fucking thick anyway. Thanks for everything. I'll never forget you. Librarians should rule the world. Michael Moore's *Stupid White Men* being pulped due to references to George W Bush, and he was only saved by a librarian. They're plotting revolution as we speak. I hope they do.

- As you do, Cortina.

- I'll miss the library and you, of course.

- What about the ones you didn't return? The

library is in a state of depletion because of you. Don't you ever think that some other people want to read as well?

-   If there, are I'd love to meet them. Now I can read the books I want, rather than the ones I have to. I intend to be artistically rich, I won't have that much money, but hey, *c'est la vie.*

-   Goodbye and good luck. You'll need it, no, seriously.

-   And to you too.

They embraced, not without a tear in both their eyes.

At that she slowly exited the room, bumping into Sr. Eucharia again.

-   You're supposed to be off the school grounds by now! Go on, go!

Cortina put on her hoodie, slung her rucksack over her shoulder and silently marched with a purpose even though there was none and would be none for some time, eyes fixed firmly on the floor, not even saying goodbye to the miscreants lining the corridor. The next step was the Three In One.

CHAPTER 4

The - Three In One- was the name of the local café, that was run by a Polish man named Kystryn. It was a relaxed place where you can buy a paper, sit down and drink a coffee if you want, or treat yourself to some religious figurines and rosary beads if you so wish, in addition to having the three in one, a specialty meal so enamored of people coming out of the local nightclubs at two am. There were items relating to the various saints, such as St Francis, St Anthony, and even the odd Pope or two. That was the most obvious reference to Catholic dogma that ever happened outside school, if that were possible. From the outset, Cortina single-handedly kept him in business. The reason for Krystn's struggle was that he refused to sell cigarettes to minors, even if they did say it was only for their daddies. He still had to make it work, being stuck on a three-year lease, hence the continuous special offers aimed at students.

Also, recently the market had expanded to include nondescript middle-aged men who would go to the café, just after the cattle mart on Friday, or air their grievances regarding their home lives.

There was a tingling of wind chimes as she entered the shop. Krystyn was quick off the mark when he saw her.

- Hello Cortina.

- Hi Krystyn, just a chicken wrap for me and a

flat white. God knows I've had a rough day.

- Why? What's wrong?

- Just got expelled, that's what. Not even a heckload of your religious figurines can help me now.

- Not even the glow in the dark ones?

- Not even the Padre Pio snowglobes. As I said, just the flat white and the wrap.

- Fine. I'll drop it down to you. By the way, this is on the house. You've had a rough day.

- Thanks. There'll be a war once I get home, this is the calm before the storm. I'm dead.

She sat down facing the window. She was transfixed by a mundane streetscape, wondering if people were going through the same mess she had, how they would carry themselves as if nothing had happened. She stuffed the remnants of the wrap into her mouth and swigged the last of the flat white and proceeded towards the door.

- Thanks Krystyn. I did get expelled. But I'm not staying around here. Especially with my dad's fiancée breathing down my neck.

- Goodbye Cortina. Good luck to you tonight. If there's any problem, come to me. I am your friend, remember?

- Thanks, but I suppose not everyone can be saved, religious figurines and rosaries and all that. There is the problem of free will.

- No chance of a cigarette behind the cigarette tree now you're gone?

CHAPTER 5

The cigarette tree was a mature beech tree, that must have been at least 200 years old and esconsed at the edge of the boys' school. It used to be on a sprawling, lush gentleman's estate which was there until the landlord gave the land for the boys' school to the Christian Brothers. It was on the cusp of an extensive car park, where the various school buses parked for the few minutes before alighting home. The students climbed onto its branches and threw butts at people. Having lit her cigarette, the first few pulls heightened her awareness of everything around her, everything was now in sharp focus.

Cortina was the only girl who was audacious enough to walk directly past the front entrance of the local boys' academy and Higgins' shop without flinching as she bought her cigarettes with impunity. She found that she got on better with boys than girls, anyway, and they would have a chit-chat and a smoke before the local buses congregated to bring the little miscreants home.

As typical, there was the mass haemorrhage of pupils from the Boys' school after the bell. The boys were more understanding of her antics, which are nothing compared to what they themselves got up to. At one time they locked a teacher in the cupboard and asked her to strip. And then, there was a time when one of the pre-fabs went on fire. No one was ever done for that. Not even Andrew

O'Connor who was always on hand to proffer a cigarette if you were stuck.

- For now, I'm okay, said Andrew. I have 100s, more ciggy for the same high price, said.

- I have six cigarettes on my person, I knew you'd like these. The teachers, for once, never frisked me. And I have a naggin of vodka for everyone. No one checked my jacket pockets. Not to worry, you can't smell it off my breath anyway. Standard procedure for going into Accounting class, the old Dutch courage.

- Got these from Germany, a box of 25 smokes for €3. Go on, have a fag, you could get hit by a bus tomorrow. Knowing your luck, it would be one of the school buses guilty as charged. Tuck in lads, she said. So that's it, you're gone from here, sighed Andrew.

- As I said, guilty as charged.

- We will miss you. You were great crack, said Denis.

- Wasn't such a great school anyway. She said.

- Maybe you'll go to a better school. Every cloud has a silver lining and all that,- quipped Andrew.

- Everyone's turning on me now. All for swiping a bloody DVD player. I didn't want it, I just wanted out.

- In fairness, it was obvious to everyone that you cut off your nose to spite your face, a deliberate act.

- It wasn't just my face I was cutting, if you catch my drift.

- What are you going to do now, Cortina?

- Take each day as it comes. There's now so much time on my hands, and I don't know how to use it. Used to be never enough time to do what I wanted, as they say, be careful what you wish for.

- Break your poor father's heart.

- Ms Masterson has taken on a lot with you two, if she's not an alcoholic by the end of this I will really be surprised.

There are serious irreconcilable differences between me and Marie. I really wish stepmothers and step-children could get divorced. Having said that, she's not my stepmother, she's my father's fiancée.

- It's all wishful thinking, the murderous fantasies.

- You got expelled on purpose, everyone knows that.

33

- How did you guess? said Cortina sarcastically.

- Not rocket science, Cortina.

- That's why you stole the DVD player.

- It's no use to anyone, not even me. I don't have the leads for it or anything.

- Going home with Marie is out of the question.

- Your ass is grass, and she's a lawnmower.

- That is the first law of the jungle – don't squeal. This town is full of skangers anyway.

- Are you really above them? Why don't you go to school, then?

- Same reason, too many skangers.

- What do you want to be?

- Happy, to paraphrase John Lennon. QED. You don't learn everything from school. This is the best education I'm likely to get. University of Life, I think they call it.

Andrew tittered.

- But in fairness, you still have to get qualifications to get anywhere. Why do you think I'm going for Law at the end of this?

\-   Not to worry. I'll work something out.

No sooner had she the words when an all too familiar red car aggressively mounted the pavement, with an immaculate handbrake turn. It was Marie with a face like a bag of spanners.

\-   I'll ignore the cigarette, Cortina, but come home. Now.

CHAPTER 6

Like she had a choice... Cortina threw the butt over her shoulder and opened the car door into another circle of hell. There was, to begin with, a thick silence, punctuated by deep purposeful sighs on everyone's part.

- Don't speak to me, I don't want to hear any tears, any excuses, nothing. Right?

- If I could get doomed on my own terms, I would be more than happy. Don't you dare take any credit for my success, or my career, come to think of it.

- If it wasn't for me, you would be facing a criminal charge. I had to wrangle with Garda Dunne before he would leave you off taking the DVD player.

- I'm fighting my own corner, the same as I have always done. Never fear. Tough as old boots.

- You wouldn't survive a week on the outside world.

- Fine. I don't want your concern, or your motherly instincts.

- Are you going to tell your father about this, or will I? It'd be better coming from you, seriously.

They turned the corner into the driveway. Dad was in the doorway with a number of spanners in his hand. Marie turned to Cortina, turning on her simultaneously.

- Well Cortina? What have you got to say for yourself? No point in telling me, talk to him.

- Dad, I got expelled. Sorry.

He collapsed into tears, violent tears at that. There and then he had the excuse of having another car to fix, even if he was in overtime and overdrive.

- Well, I am disappointed but not surprised, will you ever cop yourself on, girl? I've been called to the school enough times.

- I know you're angry, Dad. I'm sorry.

- I'm the one who's sorry, Jesus. I feel sorry for you, more than anything, which I suppose is worse. Anyway, I have to fix Tommy Kirwan's car. Goodbye.

At that, he bolted outside brusquely, as if avoiding the ominous silence casting a pallor over the kitchen. That was one thing she learned from Marie.

- Cortina wished he would say something, why is this? Why you? Why me? How can you do this to me? I'm your father, your only family! I wanted you to get an education, not this! This is worse than a disgrace, it's an abomination. I would have loved to have had the educational opportunities you had. You threw it all away.

He still had nothing to say, pejorative or otherwise. Marie had to take up the slack.

- Now you see, are you satisfied? Broke the poor man's heart. He shouldn't have had to go through this, you were the great white hope of the family, now look at you. A waster, a waste of space. Your cards are still marked, I'm still watching you, no matter where you go.

There was nothing left to do but for Cortina and Marie to watch television together, waiting for Dad to come in, to watch *Coronation Street*, as he was usually inclined. This time he was stuck outside, in what seemed like forever.

- See? See what you have done? Hmm?

- I don't care if you are engaged to my dad. We were perfectly fine until you came along. I'm warning you; you do not violate the bond between a father and his daughter. I never needed a mother figure, and you never fitted the bill. My mother's memory is sacred, OK, I never knew her and all that, but that's as far as it goes. Anyway, no mother figure would go around needling her child to the last degree about something she does not know or care

39

about. You and your bloody statistics! And for what? Make the world a better place? Coming from you, no!

- Perhaps you can do something productive with your life, helping me, for that matter, in my studies, as you said as much yourself.

- Yeah, right. How many more surveys? How many more interviews? Bloody statistics, all over again.

- Whatever about me being finished, you're finished. What will you do now? Are you going to turn out the same as Maggie Brosnan, begging and selling stolen jewellery for the rest of your life?

Maggie was a legendary homeless woman who used to sit down at the bottom of the main street, begging and selling jewellery that was obviously stolen. She often sang the opening bars of 'Nobody's Child' over and over again, much to the indifference of the locals, she was given a council house but had lots of drinking parties with her brothers and was, not surprisingly, evicted. One time, she came up to Mrs. Doran, of the local artisan bakery and laughed at her, saying 'You spent €300 to keep this place running in a week and I made the same money *today* just by begging! I get €2 a *minute* here!'. There's something to be said for milking the tourists.

- To look at her, you would know that she wasn't starving to death – she's huge!
- Don't give her anything, Cortina, do you hear

me? said Dad.

- Talk about being hung out to dry. Am I some recidivist paedophile that has to be monitored every hour of the day, even before I get out of bed? My life is a farce as it is. Now I know how the Big Brother contestants feel; only they *volunteered* to be on the show. You're just a blow-in, an old pretender. You've no business laying down the law on me. Now I have to wash the dishes, that have accumulated since this morning, in time for supper.

- Yes, washing dishes. That's all you are good for.

- Well, I have Joyce's *Dubliners* to get through afterwards.

- Finish what you've started.

- The book, yes.

- No, the dishes. After all that's happened, you have better pitch in now and again.

- Already do, without your help. Supper's nearly ready, call him in.

Dad brought in a carburettor into the kitchen, with intent to work on it that evening.

-   If the kitchen door was any wider, he would bring the whole car chassis in here.

-   Welcome to my hell, Marie.

-   Ger, don't even think of having that thing on the kitchen table, supper is nearly ready!

-   Have to get this done before Monday. Bernie McDaid wants it sharpish.

-   Why is it so urgent that it has to interfere with dinner?

Dad took the hint and placed the carburettor on the counter.

-   Go and set the table, Cortina, said Marie, - not that you deserve food.

Everyone ate in thick silence. No one dared to speak to break the tension, even if there was the odd recriminating glance across the table. There was the solemn gathering up of plates to the sink, and everyone stared at Cortina as she did so, silently nailing her to a cross of her own making, a crown of thorns pressing into her soul.

-   I'm going to my room, declared Cortina, every day has enough trouble of its own, as you always say.

-   Stay here a while, can't you?

\- Nah, sorry, Marie, I'm only fit for the bed. I said, I'm going to my room. Staying out of your way, as you wanted. Sport yourselves while you may.

CHAPTER 7

From the bedroom window, she would witness whatever was going on, with her dad on site.

Most nights, and this was no different, he had friends around him and a dismantled car, almost every evening, especially during the summer. Like a pack of hyenas devouring an animal carcass, scavenging to get parts they wanted. Right down to the tee of Marie distributing bottles of beer, that was Cortina's special job before this happened. Usurper.

- Heard about that daughter of yours, that's shocking.

- She did get expelled on purpose, didn't she?

- Wouldn't put it past her. A right bag of tricks she is.

- As complicated as a bag of ferrets, and a bag of cats to boot.

- She does ask for it, though. What's she doing now?

- Probably with her nose in some book or other.

- This particular apple did fall far from the tree. Are you sure she's yours?

- Yes, unfortunately. I wish I had the opportunity, or excuses she had to get ahead, but she doesn't care about herself, or about me, for that matter. I don't know what I am going to do with her!

- In fairness, it's worse the students are getting. There's an open revolution in the schools nowadays.

The way he dismantled engines was impeccable, in the sense that starting cars after fixing them was the cherry on the cake.

He specialised in recycled Ford car parts and this time was no different. Even if he did name his daughter after the car.

They gathered around, smoking and drinking beer, and Cortina was inclined to let them at it and not for her to interfere with their camaraderie, unless the landline phone rang for him. At least they had the good sense to switch the car off while smoking. Especially when what they were smoking were not, to her knowledge, regular cigarettes, but she was in a position to let that one slide, as long as they were in a fit state to drive home. The powers that be were scanning for drugs at every stop-and-search on the main road; just let them at it, at their peril.

There was the solemn ritual of excavating through mechanical mess that was a graveyard of used and derelict cars. Dismantling engines, carburetors, turning garbage into gold. One's poison was another person's meat. Scrappage deals were a bonanza, checking in vehicles on the cheap, if not a magnet for the odd traveller helping themselves to his ersatz gold. Because of this, he made sure that the gate was padlocked and had a shotgun at the ready on standby, just in case. You never know when the itinerants would drop by.

He knew how to dismantle cars in an environmentally safe fashion. Engine oil, and petrol/diesel were taken away and removed for further treatment and neutralisation. However, he drew the line at doctoring the diesel from tractors and selling it off to unscrupulous customers.

And then there were modern damaged vehicles bought for dismantling. NCT failures, the lot of them.

- I do regular vehicle check with my clients, it's the stock-in-trade of my business nowadays.

- The NCT was the best money spinner ever, for you.

- While it may be true that while old mechanics of cars are sometimes the cause of accidents, more are caused by some faulty nut at the wheel, but don't tell anyone that. I'm running out of room for these chasses, that's the only problem. I specialise in cleaning up problems that cause 70% of highway breakdowns. Like changing tyres or jump-starting batteries. I mean, just push the car along and it'll start anyway and keep it running. Simple as that. You'd be surprised at how many come in here with just a flat battery. Can't they rely on some Good Samaritan to pull over and do the job for them and push the car slightly uphill? What's wrong with waving a white rag to get attention of passing motorists? Or the AA? Or even hazard lights? I've seen so many cases simply because they left the radio on unattended.

- Yes! I've seen it, and I've seen it.

- I salvaged whatever material there was. Sold on old tyres to farmers to cover silage with. Those will get completely consumed. Replacing engines, carburettors and such like. Even the odd passenger door.

- Like Frank McCluskey, the Labour TD, said about the people who entered his 'clinics', the first lot want you to do something impossible, the next want you to do something illegal, and the rest are just lonely. In corrections, *most* of them want to do something illegal, like clocking, or diesel laundering, or petrol stretching. I don't deal with 'company cars' either. Have to keep my nose clean, I do have a reputation to protect.

- Could make a killing there, but you're too honest for that.

When Cortina was small, her father was terrified of letting her out of his sight, for fear that she might crawl into a car chassis just and never come out again. He kept her inside the whole time. Now he wonders what he did wrong that she ended up like this. He wished he did lose her now.

- Why is she called Ford Cortina anyway? Just

curious.

- Well, said her father, I trained as a mechanic with the promise of employment at the Ford car factory, but it closed down in 1984, just before I could have got a shoe-in there. After that he decided that if he could consecrate my first-born child to the god of automobile technology and innovation, he could charm the fuckers back to the country. The Ford factory fed, clothed and educated a lot of families in Cork over the years, can't say fairer than that.

- I mean, the closure of the Ford factory came as a shock even to the Taoiseach. One should have gone to Belgium where they were churning the feckers like smarties.

- My grandfather's car was a Mark V Cortina, salt of the earth. God, how I loved driving in that car! Even if it was a struggle keeping the inside dry. Would still be driving it, if it weren't for the NCT, didn't qualify for vintage status. I would love to see an actual Ford Cortina come here to be serviced, but it never arrives. Not so much as a Ford Anglia, for my trouble.

- Didn't go so far as to name *my* daughter after a car. Ford Sierra would have been a cooler name, come to think of it.

- Well, I'm stumped, but there are fellas out

there who love their cars more than their wives, if not their daughters. Still, it's a sin to make a joke out of someone's name. Ford Cortina? No wonder she's a lunatic. At that, I was never hot on the name Ford Fiesta, or the name of any small car, for that matter.

- Do you remember those DeLorean cars, you know, *Back to the Future*? Those that were made in Belfast? Considering how they panned out, you were lucky not to succumb to temptation and up sticks to the North. The loyalists wouldn't be happy, the people from the Republic taking all their jobs.

- Never mind. Did you see the so-called moving statue of the Virgin Mary in the factory? People used to go there and say the Rosary to herg on their breaks. It got shifted around a few times. Now it's in Mulgrave Road, where it has been for years.

- The Eleven Acre site. I've heard of it. That was where the finished articles ended up before sale.

- But these cars were better than the Ford Pinto that they had in the US, where the fuel tank was dangerously close to the bumpers. Major design fault, if you ask me. Just as well they don't sell those over here.

- I often give Sergeant Dunne, the local Garda, services to his white Ford Mondeo squad car.

You can't take chances in his job. Especially if it's a White Dublin registration car.

- I suppose you remember that song 'White Cortina'? By a Cork band called Nun Attax way back in the 1980s. Good song, that.

- 'Cork is an Anagram of Rock'? I certainly believe it.

Then the car owner, Mr. Kirwan, came along, with a hopeful look on his face. Dad knew there was trouble afoot, as he accosted him into the office. The office was a decrepit prefab, that was lit rather dimly, and was strewn with various odds and ends of disemboweled cars.

- Well, what's the verdict?

- Well, the car is totally screwed, toasted, starter, carburetor, and engine. Kaput.

- It's fucked?

- Precisely, I wasn't going to use such colorful language but yes, it's fucked. The best I can do is give a Certificate of Destruction, so it won't go back on the road. For one of these you must bring your Vehicle Licensing or Registration Cert with you. Do you have it?

- But it had a careful lady owner, even if it was fifteen years old. She looked after that car!

- It is fifteen years old, lady owner or otherwise, as I have said. My daughter is the

51

same age as that car. Has to conk out sometime, and soon. Built-in obsolescence, you understand. As I said, toast. Where's the Registration Certificate?

With a heavy sigh of resignation, he opened the glove box and took some documents out.

- Here, he said, I've really earned my money tonight. So have you.

He looked at him and turned away.

- Hey! There is some good news, though. You have four months on your tax and insurance; you can cash it in or use it against a new car. Can't say fairer than that. And here's €1000 for your trouble, that's the best I can do.

He wrote out a cheque. The man slowly edged towards the front gate, got into his own car and sped off.

- Poor creature. Look how attached he was!

- At least I'm not cannibalizing cars and sending them on to the lowest bidder. There is a thing of the Recycling Certificate for motors received. Most of those modern cars can't be hot-wired. Either that or I give them a few bob for it and send them off with a flea in their ear. I still have the tow-truck for emergencies. Thank God I didn't have to use it that often. I do have a certified weigh-bridge and scales for smaller amounts and a truck with a crane

and grab to upload heavy items. Again, I don't
need to use it that often.

- Do you remember when Mr. Walsh came in
on his Renault 20 – every week there would
be something wrong with it – fan-belt,
alternator; carburetor, starter, until he finally
copped on and bought a new car. The car
ended up on the far end of the scrapyard. We
never saw hair or hide of him ever again, but
he was a good sort!

The odd time there was petrol in a diesel engine or vice
versa, we can't help you there, just get a new engine, it's
screwed. Pity we don't deal with cosmetic surgery.

Cortina stood inside her bedroom window, witnessing
the scenario. The news was on, and she always made sure
that he would come in to see it.

CHAPTER 8

It was then, going in at the close of day, that everyone had to face the music. Marie marched up to him outside and predictably gave him the third degree. He decided to delicately broach the obvious question.

- How are things? he said, how is she? Where is she?

- She's in her room. You've been too easy on her, Ger. Too late to establish ground rules, she's a lost cause. This is as much your fault as hers. Waiting for her to cop herself on? It's just like standing in front of the microwave waiting for it to 'ping', if it ever does.

- Don't tempt me…

- Cortina marched up to the two of them.

- What was this about? blurted Cortina, I didn't even open my mouth! What did I do to deserve this?

Dad was in tears, again.

- Go to your room! scowelled Marie, now look at what your poor father. What have you got to say for yourself?

- Nothing really.

- Nothing really? Is that all? Brought shame on the family and broke your poor father's heart.

- They're not your family, they're mine and dad's.

- You were the great white hope of the family, now you're gone.

- What am I, only the daughter of a scrap merchant?

- Exactly.

- At least that daughter of yours isn't pregnant, said Marie, with a wistful air.

There was the slight twinge of conscience at that point. She suddenly wished that she was not Cortina Murray at that point. Just to be someone else, anyone else.

- Stay here in the sitting room where I can keep an eye on you. You're lethal when you're on your own. Everyone in this town's laughing at you, do you realise that?

- I should be ashamed of myself but I'm not. I know I did the right thing by me, and I'll never regret it. I'm not your daughter, or even stepdaughter. I just happen to be the daughter of the man you hope to marry. Not to worry, I've chosen for you. You're a cunt, and you're

56

welcome to him. I'm out of here. I'm going for a smoke.

- Ger followed her.

- What is wrong with you now?

- Her getting her feet under the table, that's what.

- Marie is a permanent fixture here and I want you to treat her with respect.

- She has no right to my respect. She's a cunt, end of.

- Don't use that sort of language. Anyone would think you had Tourette's the way you were carrying on.

- Just stating my case, what I think, surely that's no crime.

- She's here to stay, get used to it.

- I'm your daughter, get used to that. Not hers.

CHAPTER 9

Cortina then went up to her room again, entertaining murderous fantasies about Marie, in between reading her latest book, all the way to the land of Nod. If she had a gun, she would sink a whole magazine into her, and devil mind the consequences. Honour among thieves in prison for the fact that she 'killed my father's second wife'– that would suit her fine. Perhaps a car bomb, suffer a blow-out on the N20, being run over, or even the old chestnut of having her brake cables cut. That and slashing her tyres or burst them with sufficiently long nails. If she wished hard enough, she would get it, but she really had to obsess over it for long enough for it to happen.

In this instance she would not let her left hand know what her right hand was doing.

- Your destiny is in your hands, Cortina, you can always change a self-fulfilling prophecy, pleaded Dad.

- I only wish I was... I am not a puppet. Interview after interview, survey after survey, questionnaire after questionnaire, just so Marie can get her thesis completed. What is she doing teaching if she is so up in the world? I initially welcomed those surveys, grateful for the extra attention. This is the first time I was taken seriously, and given a free Mars bar. This is worse than what Elizabeth

Bathöry got up to!

- Who is Elizabeth Bathöry?

- She was a princess in Hungary who bled young women to death, so she could bathe in their blood and retain her beautiful looks. You do the math.

Dad could not but break his silence.

- I am glad I have no other child. I wouldn't let them so much as squeak after this. I just wish I had the opportunities that you are throwing away.

- Never mind me, who is the new guy dismantling that car?

- You won't be here forever, that's why I got in the trainee apprentice. I need a professional pair of hands to work with. Go get him a beer, while you're standing, go on.

Cortina reluctantly went to the fridge and took out some cans, and dutifully went outside. The new apprentice looked at her with inappropriate intent.

- Why don't you sit on my knee, he said, and we'll talk about the first thing that pops up?

She gave no response to that so-called joke.

- Here's your beer.

The apprentice looked at her lustfully and grabbed her by the hips.

- You are one prize heifer.

- Stop it, go away from me, you're not funny.

- It's just a joke! said Dad, every girl wants to be told how attractive she is. Some people sure can't take a compliment.

- No one who paws a fifteen-year-old and should get away with it, good apprentice or not. No decent father would allow such a person to make remarks like that about his own daughter. I'm surprised at you, dad, I am your only offspring.

- But it's only a bit of fun, Cortina! Don't you have any sense of humour?

- You know nothing about women! Being groped is not funny or fun. Being compared to an animal is beyond the pale. I am very protective of my body, and I do not want it violated in any way. Got that? I am not a piece of meat, Dad! The guy is a nonce!

- Just laugh, Cortina, he's only messing. You're too serious for your own good. Every girl wants to be told she's attractive. Why should you be any different? He doesn't mean anything bad by it.

- Don't see it that way. What sort of father would let his daughter be assaulted like this? It's unnatural.

- Just laugh, Cortina, laugh.

He groped Cortina again

- I'd love to rip your knickers off.

- I didn't know you were wearing them.

- If this car was you, I'd pinch her bottom.

- If I were a car, I'd run you over.

- Why can't you just laugh it off? You take things too seriously and you have no sense of humour.

- His so-called wit, I've heard it all before. I'm going to my room again.

At that she went upstairs, took out a book and disappeared into the pages for safety. Man, the barricades.

CHAPTER 10

She didn't get a chance to read before Marie brusquely knocked on the bedroom door.

-   If you really want to do something productive, you can help with the engagement party. Funny, this is our party and your father, and we have to provide the refreshments and food ourselves. Strange, huh? Not even give us a surprise?

-   We've already done that, with the hot food. Chicken wings, sausages, vol-au-vents. And people will be coming in with their own refreshments on a BYOB basis. This is a party after all, and it is a given that you bring your own drink to a party. Anyway, there's plenty of stuff for sandwiches if needs be.

-   Fine, now open that sliced pan for me, and get me that corned beef!

There were delicate china cups, belonging to Marie's parents being taken out of mothballs for the occasion. Cortina was strongly told not to break them as she set the tables, with other particulars being borrowed from the good hearts of various neighbours. There was almost an obscene amount of food for the occasion, arranged on a tier of plates, in addition to fairy cakes, pavlova, and sandwiches.

There was the washing of the kitchen floor, done impeccably.

- Wow! You've done such a good job on the floor! With your qualifications and experience, you should do that *professionally!*

Cortina bit her lip and kept mopping.

There was a polite knock on the door. Cortina knew who it was through the frosted glass.

- Come in, Hiram!

Hiram and his wife Eilis came in. Hiram was her mother's cousin, a solicitor with a bustling trade in town. He was married to Eilís, a librarian, who was always immaculately casually dressed and had her hair up in an untidy bun.

- How do you know these people? Asked Marie.

- He knows me well, he used to babysit me as a child, and now I look after theirs, I was godmother to their youngest child. I was the flower girl at their wedding. What we don't know about each other isn't worth knowing!

- She used to play games of 'Rodeo' with the kids on her knees and make up stories to keep them entertained. As if they don't make enough of their own fun!

- She also always brought a bag of clove rock sweets for the kids. They like that.

Eilís, sauntered into the sitting room, leaving Hiram momentarily alone.

Hiram was a solicitor and reveled in his unofficial position as a peacemaker and an ersatz son of God. He didn't leave his lawful duties at the front door of his office. Scanning the sitting room, he knew something was up, and he knew Cortina was not in the mood for celebration.

- I can't take this situation anymore, Hiram. This is insane.

- You can't go against your father's wishes. Think of his happiness.

- Well, it's not an ideal situation, to put it mildly. This is freaky!

- Just keep your head down, you'll be fine.

- I should just move to another life. I think there's more to life than this.

- No seriously. You won't last a week out there in the outside world. Not in the city, anyway, you understand.

- I fought my own corner up to now, one more crime on my part won't make much of a difference.

- I hope it's all you can get done for. Have you ever done, well, drugs, for example?

- Would it make any difference if I said yes?

- Your father is in tears, after you are getting expelled. You could have ended up down the barracks, in a police cell, and for what? Stealing a DVD player! It would have served you right, taught you a lesson. How did you think that you could get away with that? And no, we are not retarded just because we don't agree with you, as you keep saying.

- I never said *you* were retarded, just the teachers in school. It bears repeating, Hiram.

- I think this constant surveillance has made you even worse, under Marie.

- Too bloody right. I am my own special creation. I value my privacy. Like hey, I go around beating and raping kids? Spare me. I don't even sell drugs, even though that would be making a killing. If I could get my hands on the stuff – great! It would be solely for my own use, come to that. No intent to supply.

- And?

- I am entitled to my own privacy. No one seems to care about that. I wish I could vanish off the radar, start a new life. Forge something for me please! Like a passport, or something!

66

- No can do, love. Not staking my career as a solicitor on it. Hope you don't mind us bringing in another guest. She's not too far removed from your situation, so be gentle with her.

There alighted a ragged-looking girl with them, stumbling through the frosted glass door.

- Who is this nondescript creature with them? She doesn't look well. She looks ill. Get her to hospital!

Eilís stepped up to the plate.

- That's Hiram's magic for you. Every so often he picks up a miscreant from the street and gives them a bed for the night back at our gaff. I don't like the idea, but according to him, that's too bad. Shows how charitable he is.

- That girl, Eilís, what's her name?

- Some girl called Alex, a heroin addict and probable alcoholic. Remember Cortina, charity begins at home and one's home is one's castle. What is she robs the place? Or shoots up in front of the kids? If that was the case, and to prove what a Good Samaritan he is, he could at least branch into social work, or set himself up as Minister for Health or Housing.

- Speaking of accommodation, can I stay with you until the wedding's over?

- Shouldn't be a problem, I would love to have you here. Junkie permitting, of course. God knows I'm going outside for a fag, can't tolerate this anymore.

- A Huff and Puff episode? Has to be done, by your reckoning. Talk in a while.

There was a predictable tingling of glasses.

- Announcement: great that you could all come here for our engagement party. We're delighted to have ye here at this momentous occasion. Well, if the truth be told Cortina brought us together, at the local school. Make yourself known, Cortina!

- Sorry, I'm not feeling too well.

At that she gave the perfunctory wave and bolted outside, much to everyone's chagrin. She sought out Eilís on the kerb on one of her Huff and Puff episodes.

- What's with the Huff and Puff episodes that Eilís is so fond of?

- Well, whenever Eilís gets in a flap about something, and it happens rather often recently, she bolts out the back door and lights up. We are all on strict instructions not to approach her until the cigarette is finished.

What about *your* Huff and Puff episodes? In fairness, can't you at least be happy for your dad?

- If he was really my dad, he would stop this farce. Look at what he is doing to me. Fuck that, I'm going inside, need a stiff drink.

- Stay away from the drinks cabinet, declared Hiram, - unless it's for a glass of coke or some minerals. Look, please don't drink, not at your age. There's no need for a young person to drink. There are still loads to do, you might not even have had your first kiss yet. When you get older and life is more complicated, and then you need it. There's a lot going on in life that you wouldn't understand. Not at your age anyway.

- She might be under my dad's table, but she doesn't have to be under my skin. Can't I even have a little sip? I know *you* neither drink nor smoke, but this is ridiculous! As I said, I'm going inside.

Eilís finished her cigarette and was in for the kill.

- Look, Hiram, this has gone on for long enough, being the Good Samaritan that you are. Alex can stay with us tonight, but no more. I am sick of checking if all of our valuables are in the right place.

- Fair to say, Hiram, she does have a point.

69

One's home is one's castle, as I have to assert.

- No one died on my watch, thank God. If they are in a good shelter, they should be alright, however momentarily.

Eilís cut in.

- No one can serve two masters, and everyone knows his first duty is towards me and the kids. Not some junkie.

Cortina could not help but cut in.

- How did this miscreant, get to where she is today? She's sinking a lot of wine, but she doesn't seem to be under the table yet.

- Never say no to a free lunch, I guess, applies to her as much as anyone.

- Thought she was a gatecrasher to begin with.

- And she is. Fragrant vagrant to boot. I know she's wearing my perfume. Could smell it a mile off! Just sauntered into the bedroom and splashed it around. With the likes of her, I lost the count of times checking if my mother's vintage jewellery was still in their box. Not to mention my own. Some of that stuff is priceless, I don't want anyone's grubby paws on them. Pity Hiram can't see that.

- In some states in America it's illegal to be

homeless. Placing spikes under the bridges, and all that, so they can't pitch up.

- I'm the one who has to dispose of the dirty syringes and tinfoil the following morning. As long as they don't jab me, I am more than happy.

- Well, Eilis, being a librarian as you are, you live totally in the literary world. As Michael Moore, the film and documentary maker, once said, you are secretly plotting revolution, and the time is ripe and ready for action.

- You are plotting revolution yourself, kid, said Eilís. Hiram and I know you inside out, come on, we used to babysit you when you were a kid, and now you are returning the favour every other weekend. I trust you with my life, never mind our kids. I just wish Hiram would not spoil the kids in compensation for his never being there and working long hours. Like is he married to me or to his pet projects, like that loon there? Tolerating someone shooting up in the utility room! Between her toes, if you don't mind!

- I suppose that's his manner.

- I don't mind *you* staying here, Cortina, seriously I don't. Just realise our home situation right now.

- Well, you can tell them to sort out their

situation with whoever or whatever made them homeless and take it from there.

- There's enough damage done as it is. It doesn't begin when he gets a call at four am to Dubin on some mercy mission, as he did the day before my 40th birthday. He has counselled rape victims, broken marriages, abusive situations, all strictly off the record, of course. It at best, seemed odd that he wasn't here, at worst he doesn't realise the most pressing problem was right under his nose. If I try to ring him for any reason, he's always in a meeting, even if the kids are sick. I do all the running here. He just comes in and zonks in front of the television at the end of the day. Never says a word to anyone. Have to manhandle him up to bed at the end of the day. That's a typical day for you, living with Hiram.

- If it's that bad, why don't you just put your foot down? Explain what's going on.

- Nah. I do love him to bits. Too much at stake if I did walk. Anyway, that stuff about 'for better, for worse' comes into play. At this rate it's more about 'in sickness and in health' with him. He's spreading himself too thinly as it is. If it weren't for us, he's been on his fourth heart attack, realise what's at stake from his workaholism. – First commandment – yourself. You have to be selfish to survive. See after yourself or else you will lose the plot. As I always said, if he's going private, I am going insane!

- He has an amazing mental stamina. Totally unlike me. Living saint. Like when he put on those plays down in the community hall, even if his own stuff is mediocre.

- You co-direct and do set design, right?

- Yes. The one rule about set design is that nothing is impossible! You had fun there too, if memory serves me correctly. Any literary leanings of yours was fostered by me and Hiram, don't forget that. Remember *HMS Pinafore*?

- Indeed.

- He had the impeccable set design, and I did the actual directing. You remember that production of *The Bishop's Bonfire* by Sean O Casey? That was some *tour de force,* on everyone's part. You were there, remember?

- Indeed, Eilís, yes I do. Resuscitating life into the old dog.

- Then was the homecoming of the local hurling team and the refreshments afterwards. He organised all that in the local community hall. Fair play to him.

- Yes, that I remember.

- So, it's not all bad. She'll be gone by the morning, mark my words. Just have to gently bring up the matter over breakfast tomorrow. Sometimes I even wonder he really is your dad. You probably did lick your talent off a stone. Well, she didn't get that intelligence from his side of the family, to be sure. Your mother liked books all right, but she wasn't overly intellectual.

- Marie marched up to Cortina with obviously malicious intent.

- There are groups of people here who want tea!

- Yes, and?

- There are groups of people here who want tea!

- Fine, and...?

- There are groups of people here who want tea.

- So?

- Do I have to spell it out? Go to the utility room and boil kettles, now! Make yourself useful for once!

- *For Once!* Had to be the world's worst hashtag.

Cortina reluctantly arose from her seat, and into the

utility room, where at least three kettles were ready there to boil water, already plugged in. Even now, she thought nothing of the chore, at least until the apprentice came in after her.

- Come on, I know you want it, he growled, and lunged towards her.

She ducked out of the way and grabbed a kettle of boiling water.

- Don't come near me!

- Of course, you want it! I know you do! Come here!

The kettle had just boiled. That was enough. She now had intent and weaponry to match, like he did. She threw the kettle of boiling water over him. There were, hopefully, third-degree burns over the upper half of his body and howling in pain to match.

Dad came in to see the situation for himself.

- What's this about? What's going on?

- I'm sick of his antics, Dad. I do not like him groping me, I do not like him throwing lewd remarks at me, I want nothing to do with him! Every time he comes around here, it's the same story, and you think it's just a bit of fun.

- You fucking lesbian!

- What's going on here? followed Marie.
- Cortina just doused the apprentice with boiling water.
- He had intent and weaponry and was not afraid to use it.

Marie lunged towards Cortina, but in time for Cortina to grab another kettle of water from the tabletop and brandish it at her.

- Don't you dare tell me what to do in my own house ever again! You got that? This was my house long before you came here, and you have no right whatsoever to push me around! Got that?

- You had to ruin everything, didn't you?

- Don't come fucking near me!

- Fine. We won't.

Dad and Marie turned the corner into the backyard. There she overheard a seriously heated argument.

- She's dangerous! We can't keep her here! You've seen what she's capable of! You just refuse to see it!

- She's an embarrassment to me, always causes a scene of some description.

- She's crazy as a shithouse rat. Send her away where she can learn a bit of manners.

- She sees too much, and she hears too much, what am I to do? All this reading.

- Now you know what she's capable of. She's turned out just like her mother.

Cortina was even more irate, to the point of explosion as she walked up to the unfolding tirade.

- You never knew my mother, so shut the fuck up.

- You didn't either.

- Like what happened to her mother, Ger, I can't have that. What if she is hospitalised?

- Once in she'll be in and out for life. No sale, Marie.

- And if she is, so what? It's the least she deserves. Maybe if you don't take control, Ger, I will. This is worse than neglecting her; she's been overindulged, on every level. You don't pay any attention, just work around the problem. No wonder she's off the rails.

- We can't send her away! She'll come out worse than she was going in. I can't take that gamble!

- You will, because I said so. I have just the solution. I am sending her around to my aunts until the wedding is over, where she can't hurt anybody.

- I've already cornered that angle; I'm going to Hiram's!

- They already have someone staying, can't you tell? When will the penny drop with you? You're not welcome there! In my day I'd have whacked you across the behind.

- In your day, retorted Cortina, they would have burned you at the stake. How dare you send me off into the wilderness and not consult me first. That's just cheeky.

- There's a lot you would know about being cheeky...! You would go and ruin your dad's engagement party, wouldn't you?

- Like John Cooper Clarke's poem, 'Twat'? Look, Marie.

- Look at her! Butter wouldn't melt in her mouth now, would it? Far cry from a few days ago! Not so brave now, I see!

- As they say, said Cortina, if you had a brain, you'd be dangerous. And you're dangerous as it is. If anyone wants me, I'll be in my room. Just take me away from this dump, if you have to get rid of me. This marriage happening is as likely as Ian Paisley becoming Pope.

- In fairness, splitting up couples doesn't do

you or anyone any favours, especially if they don't agree with you said Dad. Marie, I think the cure you're proffering is worse than the disease. Whatever about Garda Dunne, we didn't want to saddle you with a criminal record so young in life. And with such ambitions too!

- I agree. If she were some gurrier we'd have no problem sending her to prison. But we can always scare her with the threat. Tough love. I think they call it.

Cortina sidled up to the situation, with an air of concern.

- The cheek of it! Deciding where I should go to without even asking me first! Hiram, tell them that I am staying with you!

- When you get to my age, you will understand why we take such measures, Cortina. Nothing is as cut and dried as we would like. If this got out, you would be taken into care, do you realize that?

- Couldn't be worse than what is happening to me now. I am in care, to all intents and purposes. I don't care about the drug addict; I just want to feel safe!

- What if Alex sticks a needle into you? Can't take that risk, said Hiram, shaking his head in resignation. If it was any other time, fine, but not right now, I am seriously sorry.

Cortina called out to Marie.

- Are you a cunt because you're a teacher or a teacher because you're a cunt? That's what I would like to know.

- You're a homewrecker in another sense. 75% of your misery is down to your own stupidity, Cortina, it's a proven statistic.

- It's also true that 65.78% of statistics are made up on the spot. I won't be around; I can promise you that much.

- Where would you go?

- Anywhere or nowhere. Seek my fortune. Discover myself.

- You're not doing that on my watch.

- Whoever said it was going to be on your watch?

Dad recovered from this tirade to try to soothe the situation.

- You probably think a little too deeply about things. Let's all put these things down to experience. We have to talk about your future, whatever about the present.

- Dad, I don't want her to stay here. We were

perfectly fine until she came by. You hear that, Marie?

- Look, it's for the best.

- This aunt of yours, Marie, do you know her, and how well? She could be Myra Hindley for all I know. How does Dad feel about this? Did you consult him in relation to this?

- Marie marched in and slapped her across the face, sending her glasses flying across the room.

- You had no right to slap me, Marie. Not in front of Dad. And me wearing glasses! You're not supposed to hit someone with glasses!

- I've no problem doing this in front of Dad. Everything you do is in front of Dad. Your whole life is in front of Dad. Live with that.

- They outlawed corporal punishment in schools in 1982!

- This is also strictly off the record, dearie. And I am out of the classroom, so I can do as I like.

Cortina did not feel defeated yet, picking up her still-intact glasses with hardened fingers.

- Story of my life. Are friends electric?

- I'll shove a phone charger up your ass and

then we'll find out

CHAPTER 11

Cortina went to her room. She sat in silence, resigned to whatever fate she would be subject to. When she finally got the courage to speak, she did so.

- Who is this person you're sending me to?

- My aunt Cat, she runs a tailoring and dressmaking service in town. She is working on my wedding dress as well, so I'll drop by now and again for fittings. You stay there until after the wedding. Do you hear me? Everything is above board and done and dusted. I've just been on the phone to her, so it's sorted. End of.

Dad tried to be diplomatic, but he was defeated, choking back sobs.

- Why do you have to be different to the whole town, Cortina? Sometimes I think you were put on this earth to shame me.

- Sorry to disappoint you, Dad, but don't flatter yourself.

- What have you got to say for yourself? You've just gotten expelled from school, and now this. Can you not behave yourself now, stay on the right side of the law?

- Yes, Dad, everything Hitler did was legal as well. Thought you should know that. The cheek! Arranging where I should go and stay and not even consulting me prior to the engagement!

- You're on your own, said Marie, I'm in no reason to celebrate either. Pack your bags, you're going to where you can't stir up any more trouble. I give you thirty minutes for you to get packed, and not a second later!

Cortina turned a corner too quickly and stumbled into her room and began to open her wardrobe. She pulled out a backpack, a relic of a long-forgotten school tour and studiously began to fill it to the brim with hardy essentials! They pulled out of the driveway, flanked by the grieving carcasses of cars, Marie began her spiel.

- You 'll be fine, never fear. We discussed this weeks ago, even before you got into trouble, we just put it forward. We need a few weeks to ourselves until the wedding.

By now, Cortina didn't put up a fight, it didn't seem appropriate to. She was used to Marie having the upper hand in every argument by now.

- Pitch in now and again, don't get under her feet. I will be around for the wedding dress fitting next Thursday, and I will check up on you then. And no smoking or drinking vodka, do I make myself clear? No swearing, laziness or getting in the way. You will be good as gold by the next time I see you!! A perfect little angel!

Cortina couldn't even move now. Marie made a sharp turn onto a driveway, missing the bollard by what seemed like inches. The famous aunt came out the front, opening a sliding glass door and smiling on Cortina's alignment from the car.

- Hello Cat! she said with a forced cheer.

- Welcome! she said with enthusiasm. Cortina, isn't it? Come inside! Make yourself at home!

Cortina was trying to place the woman's age; it couldn't be more than fifty. She had impeccably applied make-up, although her hair was a dignified grey, and a waft of seemingly expensive perfume announced her arrival on the front porch.

Marie was in her element, as was her won, so it seemed. She marched in ahead of Cortina.

- Take a seat inside and we'll deal with you afterwards.

There was some serious whispering. Cortina already knew what was going to be said.

- I really appreciate your help, Cat. She's got herself expelled from school. She's dangerous, she just threw a kettle of boiling water over the father's new apprentice because she didn't like the look of him. She's really freaking me and my man out. Just look after her until after the wedding, right?

Cortina mustered enough courage to ask questions.

- How long am I here for?

- As I said, until the wedding, or when you get some manners, whichever comes first. You broke your father's heart, and I can never forgive you for that.

- He was my father long before he was your fiancé. You have no claim on him unless I gave it to you to begin with, and I didn't do that.

Marie slapped her across the face and sent her glasses flying across the room.

- You abdicated any right to his fatherly love the moment you got kicked out of school. He's mine now and don't you forget it! I own his body, mind and soul. Got that?

- Leave the poor girl alone, Marie. She's got enough on her plate as it is.

- I'm not finished with her yet.

She turned to Cortina.

- Any misbehaving and there'll be hell to pay, got that? And no smoking either.

- Fine. Whatever you say.

At that, Marie turned her heel and darted out the front door, speeding out of the cul-de-sac. It was almost insulting how quickly this episode happened.

- Ah now, Ford Cortina? Is that a drag name?

- Drag name? What's that? No, it is my real name. Look, I didn't ask to come here.

- Now Cortina, not to worry. You and I will be the best of friends. Whatever about Marie, don't worry about being prim and proper in front of me, any mischief is more than welcome! Cat is not my real name either, just down to the fact that when cats go in heat, they can have two or three fathers to the kittens. So it is.

Cortina could only muster a whimper.

- What's wrong? Cat got your tongue?

- Precisely.

- You grew up in a scrapyard? Ah sure, what more do you need? Some garages would rip you off just because you were a woman, so you need to be careful. You probably know where to get the best part-worn tyres, do you? Could do with them myself. Have the NCT coming up shortly.

- I hate to say this, but I'm not a tomboy at heart. I used to clean the house and fix suppers for my dad while he was ripping apart old cars, before going to play with my dollies. Sure, I know the ins and outs of what goes on behind the chassis, but all I can really do is change a tyre. That's all people want me for. Oh, and changing the oil in a car, that too. I cook meals, keep the place tidy, gives my father his breakfast, lunch and tea, nothing special. That and supplying the lads with cans of beer in the evenings.

She looked over her shoulder at a veritable Aladdin's cave of various oddments and expensive-looking fabrics hanging in the window and diamanté jewellery, right down to the glitterball in the centre of the sitting room.

- You seem pretty certain you want to scupper the wedding, but you just don't see how. Just biding your time, eh. Eh? Well, we shall see. Let me take you up to your room, dump your stuff, and we'll see what happens after that. There are some things here that you wouldn't understand. Take everything from now on with a pinch of salt.

She took her upstairs to a brightly painted bedroom. There were murals of various flowers on the walls as well as a single bed in the corner, and a built-in plywood wardrobe. It had the smell that was typical of recently purchased furniture.

- I hear that you're a bit of a tearaway. Well, I'll

never be bored while you're around, at least, and vice versa. Maybe you and I can get along beautifully. Come and give me a hand once you've finished your tea.

Cortina mutely followed her into the kitchen.

- There's no need to walk like a board, girl! Just relax, be yourself, calm down.

- What about Marie's wedding dress? Is she coming in for a fitting anytime soon?

- Next Thursday, as she said.

- To be fair, I wasn't expecting that. You do have an interesting day job.

- I do a neat line in dressmaking, and alterations. What I don't know about dressmaking isn't worth knowing.

- Good, you're very lucky like that, handing all this expensive material and such like.

- She took a taffeta dress and pressed it against herself, looking in the mirror with envy.

- Next week, probably, I don't know. What's up with you? Relax! No one is going to bite you. Ostrich feather boas, silk, taffeta, satin, glitter, lamé. You are in a very privileged position, so milk it! At this time of year, I have hordes of eighteen-year-olds messing

89

about with these fabrics in time for the Debs ball, the more in advance the better.

- Hmmm.

- Believe me, I have enough stories of girls with your age coming in, to try on the wedding dresses, or better still, a woman in her thirties who is obviously isn't getting married, trying on the same dress she put a deposit on months before, at least every month. Did you ever see the television program *My Big Fat Gypsy Wedding*? Some of those dresses are at least seven stone in weight on their own. Like, what are they trying to prove? You've never seen such a get-up as those, fairytale weddings and such like. Those gypsy outfits wouldn't fit past the front door in this house anyway.

- Sounds cool.

- On the sly, I run a website and night called Click and Drag, catering to those men who is a transvestite on the quiet. It keeps me young. I don't have to look at the punters, just dress them up, have my wicked way with them, and they leave their money on at the bedside table. None of that 'love at first-sight' bollocks you're fed with these days. I wouldn't change it for the world. Well, you could say that I am a televangelist – commanding these repressed demons here to come out!

Cortina was stunned.

- Does Marie know about this? Don't tell me you work on the dark web!

- No. Just as well. Having said that, our shows would freak you out, not to mention the nation's grannies. Or any level of respectable society, for that matter. But you're still a bit young for all of this. That's my only concern, people going on about things that you wouldn't understand.

- Look, I didn't want to come here!

- Well, you did ask for this situation, with your dad's apprentice. But there's nothing we can do about it now. What is your game? Drugs, cigarettes, drink?

- Probably all three.

- *Probably?*

- Look, I don't know, swig some vodka, meet some boys, have a smoke. But I'm hardly quiet!

- You're not too young to take an interest in them, that's the worrying part. I hear you hang out with them by the so-called Cigarette Tree? hmm? I suppose always watch for the quiet ones. Squeaky wheel gets the grease, as they say.

-   Nailed it, so you have.

Cortina surveyed the literature on the coffee table.

-   What sort of stuff is this? *Vogue? Tatler? The New Yorker?* This is way over my head. Oh my goodness, *Playboy.* This stuff is weird.

-   Yes, as you say. But there will always be a few miscreants like you who will put a spanner in the works.

At that she winked.

-   You really are my kind of woman. What will you be famous for? Having made the journey to me? For your information, I remember when *Playboy* was banned in Ireland, but I managed to get myself a watch with the logo on it, I thought I was it!! Not that I pulled any chicks, though, as if I wanted them. The watch still works.

She proffered the watch to Cortina. It was ordinary black and white, plastic affair.

-   Have it ten years, still works, mind. If you really want, could you not read *Salon, Vanity Fair, for The New Yorker*?

-   If you have them, I'd read them. Anything as long as it's free.

-   Well in that regard you will never be bored.

Keep reading and no-one gets hurt!

- We'll see. Whatever about top-shelf pornography, they say masturbation stunts your growth. Built in convenience, come to that. Suppose you have to suffer for your art. What about your clients? And your transvestite buddies? I definitely feel as if I am in drag myself.

- And so you are. What are you doing in men's clothing? Combats and a German army jacket? You're not quite there yet but give it time.

- If you say so…

- Don't diss them out of hand, Cortina. These fairies are my babies! I pity you sometime, being - what was it? - a surly girlie. I, for one, would never want to be a teenager again. I am happier now in my own skin than when I was your age. I can be serious when I want to be, but I have developed a healthy sense of humour and I can laugh now and again, often to myself. My God, they don't make maiden aunts like they used to. What, knitting bootees by the fire? Give me a break.

- You sleep with these guys?

- Don't be so shocked! 70% of transvestites are not gay, they just like women's clothing. It also keeps me young. You can marry anyone or anything you want these days. I remember a piece in a tabloid newspaper about a homeless man who married a badger; apparently, they have a full and active sex life. Not to mention the artist Tracey Emin? She married a rock in her garden, while dressed in her father's burial shroud. Would you credit that? Never answers back or anything and you always know where he is. Perfect.

- I heard that there was a girl who fell in love with a tree and married it, after every shite boyfriend there was. Can't say I blame her.

- There was a piece in Giraldus Cambrenis' book, *Topographica Hibernia* about a man who was half an ox and an ox who was half a man. Now that happened I will never know, still makes me laugh when I wonder how it was conceived. But it's not freakish, just different. How many of the stable hands cut their sexual teeth on this sort of thing? You'll never look at cow-tipping in the same way again.

- I really do not want to know. I've bloody well heard enough. With this information I feel like the first Lady Freemason, who just happened to stumble on one of their meetings in the next room. Or like Bluebeard's current wife, stumbling on *that* room. Could they not just wear women's clothing?

- It's not that simple. You see, women are wider

at the hips, whereas men are broader at the shoulders while their hips are flat as a board. You have to accommodate these discrepancies while at the same time flattering the whole figure. Some of these guys are well ahead of me, wearing lingerie under their best suits before they come here. Of course, there's no shock value in it anymore. In a generation we will all be wearing whatever the hell we want, drag or otherwise. You know, in the early 20th century women had to get permission from the authorities to wear trousers.

- I was not aware of that. Nobody needs a permit to wear women's clothing.

- Ha! Just walk down the street at the wrong time of night and see how far you'll get.

There was a knock on the door. A respectable-looking man in a suit alighted on the porch.

- Hello there!

- Hello, how are you?

- What's your name?

- Ford Cortina.

- Like what? The car?

- No, it's my real name, and yours?

- My name is James, pleased to meet you. My drag name is Miss Information.

A stout, balding man came up beside him.

- And this is my partner in crime, Mea Culpa.

- Tonight, I am going to be a beautiful princess.

Cortina could not but cut in.

- When did you decide you were gay?

- How very English of you! You mean when did I experience the blinding flash of light? No seriously, the penny dropped long before your age, around the age of twelve. I always liked soft clothing, dressing up and such like. But I am just a transvestite, I am not gay. I can't stress that enough. For the record I am married with three kids.

- Why do you do this or dare I ask?

- It's cathartic for me, let off some steam. Suburban survival tactic.

They disappeared into the back room, modelling the creations that were hanging up inside. They had lingerie that left nothing to the imagination, revealing very hairy bodies that was for Cortina was a turn-off. This place was a BYOB affair, as she was now used to, in addition to the delicacies Cat proffered from her own drinks cabinet.

Suppose it's necessary if you were staying overnight, a half-assed excuse to the wife regarding a company meeting and all that.

- You'll have to excuse us; we have business to attend to. See you tomorrow. All of this is way over your head. Stuff that you wouldn't understand.

At that Cortina turned on her heel and was gone, with an almost trademark sulk. If Cat wanted to entertain her own nefarious guests, let her. That's her business. She chose not to let her imagination run riot about what we are going on there, in effect, she really did not want to know, enticing though it was.

It was now Thursday, and Cortina observed, it was 10pm. Marie would be going for her dress fitting anytime soon, if not now, perhaps tomorrow. She braced herself into silence for any given moment. At this stage it was late, and Marie was doing her best to take her time.

Sure enough, there was a screech of brakes in the driveway, again narrowly missing the bollard.

- Marie! What are you doing going for a dress fitting? It's 10.30pm!

- The wedding kitty. Where is it? I knew she would take it. Where is she?

- What wedding kitty?

- There's a wedding kitty amounting to €400. I

know she took it. She's not getting away with it this time, mark my words.

Marie bolted into the sitting room, where she saw a load of garishly dressed men lolling about, oblivious to the outside world, at least for the evening that was in it.

- What's going on? Who are these people? What are these faggots doing here? Come on, tell me!

- Nothing you need to worry about. This is my business, not yours.

- I wasn't expecting this! Exposing Cortina to all this! This is so fucked up, where is she?

- In her room, if I remember correctly.

Marie stormed upstairs. Cortina was nowhere to be seen, nor her meagre belongings.

- She did a bloody Lord Lucan! You were supposed to look after he, you know, until the wedding. What happened to her?

- I don't know. She could be anywhere or nowhere by now. I'll ring her phone.

A tinny ringtone betrayed itself from under a mass of bedclothes.

- She's left the phone behind her, that's not like her.

Rushing through the trees and the undergrowth, Cortina closed her eyes for as long as possible, for fear they would shine like diamonds and betray her. She surmised that her clothing would protect her, melting into the colour of the undergrowth. It was s camouflage pattern, after all. She never believed that this would come in handy until now, up to now it was no more than a fashion statement. It was damp, cold and things were barely visible, aside from the windows of the house begging her to come home. It was difficult, being outdoors and suchlike, but she had to sleep, and after that, plan her next move.

The moment she woke up, Cortina sat up with difficulty, creaking bones and suchlike. There was a stench of damp and mould pervading her miniature environment. She glanced at her watch, it was 10.15am, there was plenty of time to run for the 10.30am bus into town. Hitch-hiking was fine, but the threat of discovery was too much. She checked her pockets, having the right change for a one-way ticket, after that, who knows?

The bus came on time, and it was fairly full, and Cortina just managed to get a seat. The man beside her almost had to laugh.

- Wow, girl! Did someone drag you through a hedge backwards?

- You could say that.

Cortina furtively checked her clothes, there was the odd bramble, the smell of damp and some of those little green balls called burrs that stuck to you like velcro. There was the sensation of the phone ringing, but she knew well and just as well that she didn't bring her phone with her. That was classed as 'phantom pain', meaning a feeling that something you close to you resonates need from your body. The man next to her continued his spiel.

- Where are you headed, if you don't mind me asking?

- Actually, I do mind you asking.

- Fine. Where are you going?

- Anywhere from this, I don't know yet. Seek my fortune. Just that I am not going home, ever.

- You mean you don't have a plan? How are you going to survive in this get-up? Some girls go out to the city and are never heard from again. And nobody cares. You're just a drop in the ocean, no more about it.

At that he produced a business card.

- This is the Prester John café.

- Who's Prester John? Is he related to Elton John?

- Ha, ha, of course not. It's a kind of Christian hostel, if you don't mind the constant God-talk, it's rather comfortable. I can give you directions once we get off the bus. And if you're stuck for food, there's the Penny Dinners, you can't go hungry in this town.

Once the bus returned to the depot and the sky had cleared, Cortina went over the pedestrian bridge, left at the traffic lights, straight at the mini-roundabout, and it was on her right. She couldn't miss it. The Prester John café as she knew it by now was a large Georgian house with a fanlight over the door and wooden shutterings in every window. There was a neon sign in the ground-floor window that declared 'Jesus Welcomes You'.

She was cold, wet and starving, a perfect candidate for the likes of a Christian hostel, or the recipient of Christian charity. Even though, she had to travel light, Cortina found it difficult to drag her stuff through the door.

-   Hi what's your name? Said a woman with the softest of American accents.

-   Cor… Tina, that's my name.

-   Are you looking for a place to stay?

-   Yes, that's the size of it. Have you space?

-   Yes, we do have space. You are more than welcome. Come with me and I will show you around.

-   Why is this place called the Prester John café?

-   It was named for a legendary, fictional Christian king who was supposed to be helping Christendom in the fights against the infidel, in the Crusades. That was in medieval times. Never found him, although he did initiate a revolution in sea travel. Let's lead you up to your room.

They alighted the narrow staircase as best they could, to a large room with several bunk beds.

- I assume you want the top bunk, yes?

- Yes, of course, well spotted.

- Teenagers always go for the top bunk, without fail. Don't know why!

They adjourned to the kitchen, with an overwhelming smell of garlic and spices.

- Now what will you have? Coffee?

- A flat white, thank you.

- Coffee? Sorry, it'll have to be instant. The percolator is giving me trouble and the stuff is stale and cold. Never mind that, you must be hungry! Well, there's all you can eat here! The food is all subsidised. And all you can watch on the television.

- I'm not a big fan of food porn or gorging on television. Those things rot your brain.

- You're not from here, are you?

- Never been here before. What is your excuse?

- Well, my name is Ann, and the other guy here is Jonah, he'll be here in a few minutes.

- Fine.

- Well, Tina, Jonah and I want you to have a comfortable stay here as possible, and we want to get to know you while you're here.

- Who's Jonah?

Cortina looked around, and there he was, a tall Latino guy with a long beard and acres of tattoos on his body.

- Hey there! What's your name? I'm Jonah.

He proffered his hand, with a bone-crushing handshake.

- Pleased to meet you. What brings you here?

- Let's just say my position became untenable and leave it at that.

Jonah laughed.

- Jesus said as much, it's not where you are coming from, it's where you are going. His mission was to the world, so that through Him the world would be saved. He wasn't holes up staring at the four walls, He got out there and met people, chatted with them.

- Well, I can hardly live by example. I've turned my back on my family.

- I know the drill, Tina. I was in the gangs of Chicago for years. Name it, I've seen it, crack, heroin, I've been there, not to mention the odd killing. I once had my best friend die in my arms, and my pregnant girlfriend as well.

- How did you end up here?

- Well, when you try to unravel your own mystery, you're like a kitten in a ball of wool, the more you struggle, the more entangled you get. That's when you need outside help, namely Jesus. The final straw came when I was hospitalised for gunshot wounds. The hospital chaplain gave me a Bible and I took it from there. When he mentioned to me about a new life as a missionary in Ireland, I jumped at the chance. I even took the new Christian name of Jonah, after the unwilling prophet. Suited me to a tee.

- All of this seems like coincidence.

- There's no such thing as coincidence. God brought you here.

- What's your situation, Ann?

- I am a recovering alcoholic.

- Doesn't sound good but go on.

- There was a time when I could down a full bottle of Jack Daniels on my own, give or take day or so.

- How did you end up here?

- I suppose God wanted it that way. It got to the stage where I lost everything, my job, boyfriend, family, self-respect, so I went to the local AA meetings and never looked back. I was one of the lucky ones, some died out on the street. I know one girl who died of double pneumonia, and she was three months pregnant at the time. All because of drink. I have loads of stories about situations like that. I don't want to see you go down that road, take the pledge if you have to!

- Not good. Sounds tragic.

- Anyway, Tina, what brings you here? You definitely need God at a time like this. You ran away from home, what's your story?

- Nothing I want to talk about. My story is nothing as exciting as yours.

- We'd really like to get to know you while you are here. Tell us your hopes, dreams, everything!

Cortina was flattered by the surge in attention but was

wary enough not to let it show. Although she was flavour of the month with this crowd, she knew perfectly well to be on her guard.

- You're a bit young to be striking out on your own, though. How old are you?
- Fifteen and a bit, no less.

- Perhaps you are on loan to the devil until a certain time. Young devil, old Saint, as they all say. There's no room for spite or bitterness here. Remember, you are on Christian ground.

- I could never aspire to such dizzy heights of salvation.

- You don't have to. We were given a free gift of salvation at baptism, so we are not called to be, but to remain saints. God doesn't manifest through the outlandish, rather through our day-to-day lives.

Ann's words came as a minor revelation to Cortina. This was one voice worth listening to. It certainly beat all she learnt at school, where they skirted around the major issues. And it was certainly an improvement on what Marie had to say for herself!

Jonah cut in.

- Salvation is something we can all aspire to. We all need some big-brother type who will stick up for us when we are in trouble, like

Jesus, come to think of it. The kingdom of heaven is within you. Not some airy-fairy kingdom in the sky. Or some half-assed desert so beloved of early Christian ascetics. This urban jungle is a latter-day desert, like Sceilig Michael. You could walk the length and breadth of this city and still talk to no-one, and no-one seems to care. You're still on your own.

- Well, I have enough money to tide me over for the next while.

Ann approached Cortina, as if to instruct her to be quiet.

- Shhh... don't say that too loudly. Some people are going to get money off you by fair means or foul. The love of money is the root of all kinds of evil. St Paul, said that, to the best of my recollection.

Cortina took Ann's admonishment to heart.

- I'm sorry, loose lips sink ships. I'll shut up from thereon in. Suppose there is something to be said for the vow of silence some religious orders are so fond of.

- Not to worry, it's fine, said Ann. You're forgiven. Just saying for your benefit.

Cortina took another swig of her coffee and looked around her situation.

- Funny, she said, CS Lewis once said that the only thing that stopped him from being a Christian for so long was the Christians themselves. But you're ok, I like you. I suppose I can trust you, come to think of that, and at present I can't say that about many people in my life. Even if I did gatecrash this joint.

Ann was now in her element.

- There are no such things as gatecrashers to God's party! Everyone is welcome.

- You're on planet earth, there's no cure for that, so said Samuel Beckett.

Cortina finished her flat white. Ann kept on talking.

- Oh yes, just so you know, let me tell you, there's the problem of taking in the surplus from the homeless hostels uptown. We may have to put them in your room, if needs be. Is that ok?

- It's not surprising you are so sympathetic towards drunks, given your situation.

- Worse it's getting. The government is dragging its heels on the issue. Do you know that there's around 3000 homeless people in this country and it's the likes of us who have to take up the slack? That is criminal, but when push comes to shove, we have to have to turn them away.

- While on the subject of alcoholics, you will have to share your room with a woman called Monique tonight. Not to worry, she's not violent or anything, she'll just snooze the night away, although she does know how to shore.

- Who is Monique creature?

- Pretty tragic creature, so to speak. She was a French woman, married to one of the richest men in the city and lost it all through drink. Her family tried to get her on various treatment programmes, but she kept absconding. Now she's on her own. But you will be fine. She doesn't stick around without drink long enough to get the DTs, or to get violent. Rather placid, under the circumstances. And elegant, to boot.

- As long as she doesn't glass me, I should be fine. Or swipe my cash. I for one am sleeping with all my clothes on and all my valuables on my person.

She was there and then, anxious to change the subject, or at least remain on the original path, narrow and straight though it may be.

- What's the trouble with atheists, what's going to happen to them?

- Their problem is that they have nothing to base their code of practice on.

- You mean a charter? Like the Magna Carta? Is there a definitive handbook?

- Maynooth is the worse for churning out atheists. Look at the study of Theology 101 if you don't believe me.

- The name Prester John, what's the story regarding that. Why name the place after some Christian king that never existed?

- Well, as the Rolling Stones once said, you can't always get what you want, but if you try real hard, you might get what you need. That's the story behind the name. Past is past. Press ahead.

- You're right. No-one who puts his shoulder to the plough but looks back is fit for the Kingdom of God. You've no place to lay your head unless we give it to you, as you were saying. Like the search for Prester John.

- Each day has enough grief of his own. What's on television?

They turned the corner into the sitting room, with a plasma TV and remote, with the old chestnut that there was 600 channels and still nothing worth watching. Cortina switched on the television. As luck would have it, it was in the local channel and this is was the local

110

news.

- What the bloody hell is going on here?

There was her dad, Marie, and Sergeant Dunne at what seemed like a press conference, a television appeal. Her father seemed to have aged ten years with the predictable heartache that came with worry, while Marie dabbed her eyes where it was obvious even to the trainee eye that there were no tears. Cortina was flattered she made the evening news, local or otherwise.

- We're worried about you, Cortina, please come home!

- It doesn't matter about the wedding kitty, please come home! We love you! We miss you!

The press conference finished as quickly as it started, with Dad getting up and quickly exiting the studio, leaving Garda Dunne alone together. The camera was still running, unbeknownst to those two. What was that between those two, flirting, affection…? It was apparent that he was looking for a case under his belt, but this…? The two being best of friends, perhaps? Good for them. The camera rolled on.

- Not to worry, said Garda Dunne, did she take any money on her travels?

- Just the money we were saving for the wedding.

-   How much was that?

-   Around €400.

Dunne was once again in his element.

-   Once the money is gone, she'll be back with
    her tail between her legs. The Prodigal
    Daughter, I should think. I have seen all this
    before. She has too much time on her hands,
    getting expelled from school. If there's not a
    sign of her after a month, then you can panic!

Marie was more circumspect.

-   That's grounds enough for her to be taken into
    care. Or psychiatric assessment. There are
    enough fucked-up people in the world besides
    her adding to the mix. I'm not finished with
    her yet. She's on the waiting list for Dr
    Broderick for long enough.

At that he gave her a kiss and was gone. Cortina looked
at the television again, with intent.

-   At least I can pronounce the word
    'committee' correctly.

Ann sauntered into the living room, and immediately
spotted what was on the television. She made it obviously
that she was looking over Cortina's shoulder.

-   Oh dear, is that you on the television? Your
    photo? That is you, isn't it?

112

- For your purposes, no.

- Really? I don't think so. It's uncannily like you, that photo.

- Well, to quote Brendan Behan, they tried me in my absence, they found me guilty in my absence, they sentenced me to death in my absence, so they can bloody well shoot me in my absence. I have renounced family, occupation, friends to forge my own path in life. I wouldn't have gone if it was better to stay at home. I am the perfect candidate for the Christian religion, in that I hate family, friends and everything else, taking up my bespoke cross every day. From my reading, all Jesus Christ said about families was: leave them. I want nothing to do with my relatives, through marriage or otherwise. I'm on my own, and I quite like it that way, unencumbered by attachments.

- That's fine said Ann, but we can't see you preaching the Gospel on street corners, laying hands on the sick, or suchlike. Jesus didn't start His mission until he was thirty. You have all this time to play with, use it wisely. Have fun, I mean it.

- Funny, Virginia Woolf said the same thing, that no one should publish anything until they're past thirty. What chance have I got?

- Sometimes I think you would be better off sitting down and watching *The X Factor* now and again, to say nothing of the soap operas. Throwaway slush-pile stuff. It might help if you didn't take things so seriously. There's no evidence that life is serious. No-one gets out alive anyway.

- I made my dad's choice easy; either her or me. If he's pining away after me it's his own fault.

- Only the innocent suffer in a war. The Bible says: 'Honour your father and your mother'. They are worried about you, I know they are. I won't rat on you, but maybe you can come to your own conclusion about this. Just do the right thing. Listen to your conscience.

- All Jesus said about families was, any person who loves their family members more than him is not worthy of him.

- They'd still be worried about you.

- I'm a criminal in the making, so says everyone.

- But, Tina, it's not where you come from, it's where you're going! You know that better than anyone. But you can stay here for the next few nights, it's no problem. Things are pretty Spartan here, but you'll be okay. Just until you get back on your feet.

- Thanks. Christian duties don't cover second marriages or at least, Dad's. She's not my stepmother, she's my father's fiancée. I can't say that often enough. Anyway, freedom is just another word for having nothing left to lose; that's Janis Joplin for you. Or even Woody Guthrie, 'If Jesus came down again, we'd nail him up again'. I must say, Jesus was very lucky there were no Christians in his day, they'd have strung him up before the Pharisees had a chance.

- Don't say that. Jesus died once for all our sins.

- He was a Jew, and the upper-crust Jews got pissed off with him. That is bog-standard alternative theology - you do the calculation. He's being crucified all over the world, listen to Amnesty International if you don't believe me! Or the Six O'clock News!

- Are you saying Christianity is useless?

- Not at all. To quote GK Chesterton, 'Christianity has not failed; it has not succeeded because it has not been tried'.

- That's a great quote!

- To say nothing of the whiskey priests this country is so fond of. As Kinky Friedman said, 'They Don't Make Jews Like Jesus Anymore'.

- These things are sent to test us. God wanted it that way.

- A life untried is not worth living. Don't know who said that, but it's true.

- Well said.

- The hatred of Marie is the only thing driving me forward, even more than the will to live.

- That's unfortunate. We have some work to do with you. Steer you in the right direction. When we forgive others, we set ourselves free. You can't spend the rest of your life hating people; if you cannot forgive them you can't go to heaven.

- Fine.

- Well, if you're serious about staying here for the next while, maybe you can join us for prayer later. Around eight o'clock perhaps? We'll be in the back room.

- Fine.

Cortina turned into the back room, with a discarded Bible in her hand.

- Now, as we all begin with Bible classes, we start with a prayer.

- We thank you, O Lord, for Tina, thank you for

116

bringing her here to stay with us for the foreseeable future. Pray that Tina will see the error of her ways, soften her heart towards her family, steer her on the right path. We also pray for Monique, in the hope she sees the path of right living sooner rather than later. And now, Ann, take it away!

Cortina couldn't understand why Ann kept pinching her on the shoulder.

- Hate! Come out of her! Soften her heart towards her family. May the parable of the Prodigal Son enlighten her! Demons! Come out of her! Unclean spirits! Come out!

It was followed by Jonah praying in tongues. That was freaky. It was supposed to be a gift of the Holy Spirit, but why would God pick this particular gift as a brownie point was totally beyond her. Freaked out as she was, she politely edged towards the door and proceeded to bolt towards the bedroom.

What was that? Clowns and jokers at every angle, not just left and right. If all else fails, go to bed. The comfort of sleep, the natural legal hallucinogenic was too much. She needed peace and plenty of it. If Monique started making noise or snoring, Cortina would not be responsible for her actions. So much for Christ being the Prince of Peace! He came not to bring peace but division. Anyone who read the Gospel would know that. But that was too much for anyone right now.

As luck would have it, Monique remained relatively quiet

for the whole evening. However, she repeatedly wet the bed over the course of the night, mumbling in French the whole time. There was a pungent smell of urine across the whole room. This militated against Cortina trying to keep all her valuables on her person, which made for uncomfortable rest. She knew enough that any form of addiction rends you selfish, in that you don't care who you hurt as long as you get your fix. There was nothing she would put past this sorrowful drunkard.

The following morning, Cortina, somewhat chastened by events in a bizarre sort of way, was approached by Ann. She seemed as flummoxed as she was, milling about with her house-keeping duties.

- Well, Ann, it's been fun, but I really can't stay here; I have to go and seek my fortune. I'll always remember you. Thanks for everything.

- Where would you go to?

- Anywhere or nowhere.

- Just mind yourself. The peace of Christ be with you always. By the way, I have something for you.

At that she produced a tiny wooden cross, on a leather thong.

- Carry your cross every day and you'll be fine. Do remember me.

-   By the way, my name isn't Tina, it's Cortina, after the car. But you can call me what you like.

At that she turned out the door and she was gone.

CHAPTER 12

It was a badly lit road, caked in mud and black sheets of rain. There were no lights on this stretch of road, or at least, were dimmed to save electricity. What was one to do? Where to go? Keep walking and no-one was going to get hurt. It was just a process of putting one foot in front of the other, it was that simple and that hard.

She crossed the road, not expecting what would happen next.

It was a pothole, and a huge one at that. It was of a size that would encumber her whole body, a type the more discerning motorist was sure to avoid. She was afraid to raise her head for fear of her head getting crushed by a passing car. Her knee was busted, and she was in serious pain.

- Somebody help me! she wailed.

She heard footsteps a short distance away. Was this a saviour?

- You all right, love? What's up with you?

- I fell into a pothole and I think I busted my knee. I'm in pain, help me please!

- Not to worry. Come in a while and I'll sort you out. Don't make it worse, take your time coming out. I'll help you.

He offered his hand to help her up and draped her arm over his shoulders. They turned to face his house quick couldn't be more than twenty paces away, but in her situation, it was more like a hundred kilometres.

- Steady on, girl, take your time.

They approached his front door, as best they could, coming in two abreast, and not in single file, as was wont for road safety.

- Breda? Give me a hand with this girl.

Breda observed the situation with disdain, as if she had seen it several times before.

- All right, love, go into the sitting room and we'll sort you out. My wife Breda is a trained, qualified, experienced nurse, she'll look after you.

Breda knelt beside Cortina and poked around her knee.

- What's the story here, Dermot? It looks pretty bad, there is some ligament damage, but no broken bones. You'll live, and you'll recover, but don't let that get in the way of a good story.

- Good story? What's the story?

- You're not the first person to trip into that pothole. There are no lights around these parts, or at least those that were of any news. It's the council's job to fix those and they haven't been down here in years! There's an election coming up soon; I thought the various political parties would move heaven and earth to fill them up, just in time for the general vote. Bastards.

- I feel so stupid, sorry, Dermot.

- Don't be sorry! You're in luck, me and you. You're the first non-relative to have fallen into that pothole. You're in the money, big time! At least €10,000 into your hand! It's the easiest money you ever got! I tell you, it's official! Ireland is the best place in Europe to have an accident. My eldest can fit his entire body into that pothole. It stood to him as well - look at that!

He pointed to a newspaper article in a frame, called 'A Boy Named Sue'; a kid on his third compensation claim. This was the same kid who was playing mercilessly on his Xbox in front of everyone.

- I like the sound of that, remarked Cortina, being temporarily elated. How do I go about this? Have to go through a solicitor, obviously.

- The solicitor is in waiting, McLaughlin. Stay here tonight and we'll send things tomorrow. Tell him Dermot sent you!

- You're sending me to an *ambulance chaser?*

- Most solicitors are two floors up some Georgian building, out of harm's way, on Washington Street, or the South Mall.

- How am I supposed to get up there on crutches?

- The more crippled you are, the better your case. Stay with us overnight and we'll see how fixed you are in the morning. You're hardly a walking wounded case, you're the real deal. Go to sleep; Breda will show you to your room. Here's some crutches to help you on your was. No hurry, I'll be right behind you, take your time going up and don't crack your skull. Steady on there.

They alighted on the landing, making their way to the next door on the right. The bedroom had plenty of mod cons, even a little palatial. The firm mattress, the electric blanket! The deep like carpet! What a residual heaven! And who told her that money could only be obtained by hard graft and tenacity? If that was the case, the women of Africa would be millionaires. They don't teach you that in Geography class.

CHAPTER 13

The following morning, Cortina made a point of coming down to the kitchen at 9am, and not a second later. It was basic courtesy, after all.

- You found us ok? How did you sleep?

- Do you have any paracetamol left? I think it is worn out, it's still a bit sore.

- Breda? Give this girl some paracetamol while you're standing.

Breda opened the cupboard, took out a tiny container and dispensed the medication. Cortina swallowed it with the remnants of her breakfast orange juice.

- Toast?

- I'm toast as it is. But thanks, I will.

- Not to worry, you can go anywhere with this story, you're a genuine case. The car's ready, so you can be on your way.

He dropped her off at a terraced redbrick house, not far from the center of town. He parked illegally for a few seconds, enough for Cortina to observe the Herculean effort to navigate the stairs.

- Here it is. Good luck, girl, and work those crutches!

- With the help of God, yes?

Once she had maneuvered the few flights of stairs, she noticed that the door was ajar. She poked her head around the door. A shadowy figure answered the door, looking male but with the squeakiest of voices. Who was this person?

- Sorry, is this McLaughlin the solicitor?

- Sorry, next door, goodbye!

He slammed the door brusquely. It was almost insulting how quickly the episode occurred. She alighted the stairs, but this time the shadowy figure opened the door.

- How rude of me! Slamming the door on you! Let's help you up those stairs!

At that he put his arm around her waist and led her along to McLaughlin's office.

- Thanks.

- No bother, he said, by the way, good luck with *him*.

At that, he smirked.

The door was slightly open. Looking inside, there was no-one but the charwoman.

- Are you looking for Michael McLaughlin? He's not here, in fact he's never here at 9am on a Monday. Comes in here when it suits him. I know because I'm here on the dot, six days a week just to clean the place. Can get very dirty if I'm not here! I come out of necessity and not because of the dirt on the windowsill. He never lets anytime come between him and his early morning tipple.

- You're telling me he's an alcoholic?

- Pretty much. As they say, 'An alcoholic is someone who drinks more than his doctor', to say nothing of solicitors. Thank God there are no alcoholic dentists, no, seriously.

- Is he a functional alcoholic?

- He's a member of the Dipsomatic Corps.

- Where's his secretary? Surely he has a secretary?

- Nah, there's a high turnover of secretaries in this joint, most having been passed and sexually harassed to oblivion. He only employs good-looking women, and with nerves of steel at that. One time he was caught *in flagrante delicto* with a woman in this office.

- What does that mean?

127

- He was caught in the act of having sex with a woman, right here, as it happens. Apparently, she was desperate to get off a drink driving charge. Didn't get it, though. She'd have been better off shagging the Garda who stopped her, to begin with. I have heard that you haven't lived until you have had a Garda in the back of a squad car, and I have no reason to disbelieve it. Would save on legal fees. All this is second nature to me, girl, and I am as silent as the grave.

- Fine.

- Anyway, what's your story? Let me guess - compensation claim? I could tell, you look crippled. You, yourself climbing those stairs as if they were Everest, poor thing. It's not often they get genuine cases like you. How'd you hurt yourself anyway?

- Tripped and fell into a pothole, busted my knee. I can show you the bandages underneath my jeans if you want. It happened on Harold Street.

- Same pothole the Duffy's keep falling into? That road is well beyond repair. They should just dig up the whole street and sort it out for good. I think the problem is with an underground stream that continuously messes up the whole street. Anyway, there's an election coming up soon, they will try to patch it up and sharpish. It's conveniently located outside the Duffy's house, they fell into it, got compensation. The judge assessing the case said 'So, alright, there's a pothole outside your house, you fell in, your wife fell in, your children fell in, you know we might as well name the whole street after you!'. Well, I will tell you why Jesus wasn't from Ireland. Why? Because He fell three times and never sued for damages. No foal, no fee. The Yellow Pages is full of them. Take your pick. What is your name?

- Cortina Murray. If McLaughlin isn't here, why are you here?

- Earning my money, so I can leave my husband.

- Never mind me, what's *your* name?

- I am the Invisible Woman. That's all you need to know.

- Why? Surely you have a name?

- Like Cortina is your real name? Give me a break.

- Why do you say that? It is my actual name, as I am sick of explaining.

- Well, as I said, I am saving up to leave my husband. McLaughlin has never been the same since his wife walked out on him, wish my husband would work the same magic and flee.

- Right...

- And to that effect, McLaughlin always pays me in cash, under the table. And all this goes into this foolproof strongbox until the appropriate time. Once I have enough saved - goodbye!

- Where would you go?

- Never mind that, I've got that angle covered, never fear. And you know what the worst thing is? My husband wouldn't even notice. Propped up in front of the television, plaintively asking for a beer. No attempt at conversation.

- Why not just get a divorce? You could easily pick that solicitor's brains or do it online without a solicitor.

- You're right, I could nearly set up a practice myself. But it's too much hassle. It's not worth my while, for all the years that are left in me. You have your whole life ahead of you, unlike me. Take my advice - don't ever get married. It's either convenience or death. Take your pick. Anyway, it's your funeral.

- Have you any kids?

- None, thank God. Promise me another thing, don't ever have children. They hijack your body for the first nine months and your bank account and sanity after that. Believe me when I say that I have seen several couples who regret having children.

Cortina thought about the Invisible Woman, as she went on her way to dusting the windowsill, how she had harboured dreams of love, of acceptance, of being wanted by someone. She pictured the husband calling plaintively for another beer, half-zonked out in front of the television, oblivious to the fact that she would no longer be there. She pictured the note she would leave behind saying adieu, the clockwork creature having sprouted wings and flown. The husband would die of neglect, but that was too bad.

- Oh, Jesus, that's him. I'm going out sharpish. Good luck with the claim.

At that she turned the corner and vanished from view. There was a drunken thud, thud, on the staircase. McLaughlin themed the corner abruptly, somehow not falling over himself and keeping his trademark lascivious nature in check.

- Hello sweetie, what can I do for you?

- I fell into a pothole and I busted my knee. That's it in a nutshell. And I am looking for compensation.

- Do you have an appointment?
- No. The charwoman let me in.

- How old are you?

- Fifteen and a bit.

- And where are your parents? You can't fight this case on you own.

- What? But - I have no parents! I'm an orphan!

- No, you're not. This isn't Victorian England. Where are your parents?

- I'm an orphan by persuasion. That's all you need to know.

- Ha! I love that! Orphan by persuasion! Well you, I've learned much terminology in my training for this job, but that is a new one on me! Who sent you here?

- The Duffy's, from Harold Street. Dermot and Breda.

- Distance yourself from that crowd, it'll prejudice your case. And bring your parents next time you see me.

The promise of riches evaporated just like that. Cortina should have known it was too good to be true. Being suitability miffed, she maneuvered her way towards the door and onto the landing, navigating, as best on

132

crutches, the best way to not crack her skull.

She saw the shadowy man's door again and approached with due of curiosity.

- I came around to apologize. I was looking for McLaughlin.

- That's the only time anyone comes here, to call into McLaughlin's. Let me guess - compensation? He's the world's worst ambulance chaser, and the laziest, come to that.

- How does he survive?

- Certain means and certain ways. That's as honest as I can be.

- Okay... I just wanted to apologize to you for barging in on you earlier. And to say thank you for helping me up those stairs.

- Well, I suppose if you came for breakfast, you might as well stay for dinner. Nothing here is too fancy, mind. I am not used to having visitors here, so I will just have to see what is in the kitchen cupboards and the fridge and work from there. Ah! I can offer you a banana, an orange, or some rice pudding.

- Rice pudding is fine.

- You're not from around here, are you?

- How can you tell?

- I can spot the weakest of rural accents at fifty paces.

Cortina knew there and then that she was in safe hands. There were books strewn across the flat, and she could not help but help herself to the rich pickings the flat afforded.

- Good flat you got here, if a bit messy.

- Yeah, I bought it before the house prices went nuts. I was very lucky then. Nowadays on the continent €1m will get you a plush château with grounds and a swimming pool in the south of France, or it can get you a shoebox in Wilton. Take your pick.

Cortina took the time to familiarise herself with his belongings, having the childish habit of picking up things and examining them, even if they belonged to someone else. There were trinkets from long-forgotten bus journeys, invaluable books such as *Catch 22, The Naked Ape, The Selfish Gene, One Flew Over the Cuckoo's Nest,* and the odd Hemingway. There were numerous collections of poetry, most of which were signed by the author, addressing themselves to this poor miscreant.

- Leave my books alone. I haven't finished with that one yet!

- Sorry, I can't help it, I love books!

- Sorry for what? Barging in on me or going through my books? But I see where you are coming from. So, I forgive you. Read whatever you want while you're here. Make yourself at home. I could do with the company. What's your name?

- Cortina.

He laughed.

- As in the car?

- My father was a mechanic, it suited his purpose, and you? What's your name?

- Philip.

- Oh come on, she laughed, you're fooling no one. Your voice is a dead giveaway. You're a girl!

- Well, let's just put it like this. I was born a male, but I wasn't born a male.

- You're saying you're transgendered?

- Pretty much, yes.

- Jesus, it's all right being a butch lesbian, but this is taking things to another level! Why do this to yourself?

- People say that God doesn't make mistakes

when I mention it to them. This is the same God who creates paedophiles and psychopaths. Now that's what I call mistakes. I have to do this to make my stint in life more tolerable. I want to live my life as a man, and if I die let me at least be valiant in the attempt. That's the purpose of the hair dye on my hands and arms - the appearance of more hair, and dark, at that.

- You up for phalloplasty?

- No, more trouble than it's worth. Most guys are not perturbed by that, about penis size, that's all down to the media. If the truth be told, there is an inverse proportion between size and technique. The smaller man has to be more inventive, make up for whatever he lacks in size.

- Not to worry, stuff like that doesn't blow my mind anyway.

- Thanks.

- Believe me, it's nothing I haven't seen before. I was sticking it out with a relative by marriage when I realised she was running a salon for transvestites. So, you're totally cool by me.

She took a deep breath.

- Why are you stuck here? Why are you alone?

- I wore my brother's tuxedo to family christening, and they threw me out. What's your excuse?

- My dad got engaged to a teacher from my school, who makes it her job to put me under surveillance for the rest of my life. I got expelled from school and I have been on the run ever since. How do you stick this place? Sick building syndrome, that's what's wrong with you.

- Ah, come on, it does the job, it's relatively neat and tidy. You are obviously a runaway, don't know the harder edge of existence but learning fast, in enough time to be reunited with your Mum and Dad, no harm done.

- Er, not exactly.

- For your information I started on the hormones three months ago. You can tell my voice is changing already, although I don't have a proper beard as yet. Still have to deal with these breasts, the sooner I am doing of them the better. It's not so much a rebellion as an act of survival. I was born in the wrong body, that's what's wrong. But you're fine here, nobody's going to bite you. Desertion by persuasion, maybe? Do I get a finder's fee like some of those soft-porn magazines do? Maybe even a reward for information? Or locating you?

- Don't you fucking dare! I might have known you for a few minutes, but that doesn't mean I am your property. Perish the thought!

- 24-hour surveillance, eh? Good reason to bolt, I couldn't stick it myself. But in fairness, you at least have a family who cares about you and is worried about you. What have I got? My folks want nothing to do with me. Apart from my brother, Brendan. He was grateful to have a younger brother, in the end.

- Are you going to grass on me?

- Not for the socially respectable rebellion, no.

Cortina was hurt to the quick.

- How dare you assume my motives to be anything less than genuine? At least your folks don't follow your every move.

- Don't know. Can you tolerate me at my most average?

- I desire mercy, and not sacrifice. What was your name, before you transitioned?

- Rather not dwell on that, that's all you need to know. Even as a child I preferred to pitch in with my dad outside, rather than do all the so-called cushy jobs with my mother and sisters. I lost count of the times I screamed when they put me in a dress, as if they hadn't prior warning I was transgendered. But don't mention that in public, that's all I ask of you. I am sick of having to explain myself to everyone I meet, being born in the wrong body and all that. I live in fear of being found out. Do I look that feminine to you, Cortina, do I?

- You look male enough, perhaps even tomboyish, but your voice is a dead giveaway. It almost sounds like Truman Capote in reverse, cracking under the weight of hormones.

- I still have problems going swimming, I wear a t-shirt and baggy trunks, not Speedos, and bind my breasts down tightly. You have to understand the subterfuge is incredible. You have no idea what I have to go through every day, but I wouldn't want it any other way. This is my identity, suffering double-takes on all levels, I feel cheated. Like when I come out of the shower and see it's not a male body.

- Now things are changing, are you happier?

- Absolutely, yes.

- Can you live scared your whole life? You shouldn't be punished for something that wasn't your fault. There's no excuse to be lonely. Come outside for coffee, if you don't believe me, my treat.

-   Might take you up on that.

Cortina couldn't help but look over Philip's shoulder at his Facebook page on his laptop.

-   You're not short of contacts, I'll say that for you.

-   I'm everyone's best friend but nobody's sweetheart.

-   If all your friends are Facebook friends, you don't have any. Do you mind putting on the television, two seconds?

She descended on the television, which was showing a rerun of *Bosco*, nothing else. Cortina breathed a sigh of relief.

-   God be with the day when you could make and do with nothing else but some pipe-cleaners and some Pritstick. You remember those?

-   Now you're really showing your age.

-   As I said, reruns! I can hardly remember *Bosco* first-hand. That was right up there with *The Elephant Show* and *Sesame Street*.

-   What's wrong with *Sesame Street*? I always watch that first thing in the morning. But never mind, let's start with a trip to the park!

They ambled down the staircase, as best as it was possible with crutches. Philip took his time, the gracious creature that he was, as Cortina navigated the hallway as best she could

- This shouldn't matter, the transgendered thing, not from where I'm coming from, anyway.

- It does matter, Cortina. I have to face this stuff. But you've come with me and no-one has said anything. They don't say it, but I know what they're thinking. All those double-takes searing into my brain, second-guessing what is wrong with me.

- I'm sorry to hear that. That's an awful cross to carry.

- But whatever about me, I won't grass on you. You're, you're too, shall I say, special and not in a bad way. I'm not a natural recluse, after all, and I suppose what I am doing here is no good for anybody. I could do with some friendship. Let's go for a picnic in the park!

- Would be delighted to. Let's go!

- Let's take the handmade throw, that was a present from my mother when I first started college: don't spill anything on it, please! Go to the shop and get some Taytos and Coke!

- Why, of course!

- No alcohol, of course, this is a public park, right in the city centre. They won't tolerate it. Even the winos have to behave themselves. The rule of thumb is: don't bother anyone and no-one will bother you.

They lay down on the picnic blanket, greedily unpacking the Taytos, and a large bottle of Coke they had bought between them, in a perfect bubble of their own. At this point, they were both young, free and easy, yet to be battle-scarred by the harsh hand of experience, although that would come.

Philip smelt so sweet, the expensive aftershave working its magic. He ran this hand through Cortina's long dark hair, occasionally snagging on her glasses.

- What do you want to be, more than anything else in the world? Philip asked.

- Freedom to be myself, surmised Cortina. Didn't get that at home, that's why I bolted.

- Same here. That's why my family kicked me out. It was either that or suicide, whichever was most convenient for everybody.

- Snap. I needed space and plenty of it, not to mention freedom. Now that I have it, so what? What's next on the agenda?

- Just be yourself, said Oscar Wilde. Everyone

142

else is taken.

- If I did that, the whole world would cave in.

- Don't flatter yourself. No-one is indispensable. If you died tomorrow, there is always someone ready to take your place.

- Someone once asked John Lennon what God he believed in, and he said, 'I don't believe in God, Buddha, or even the Beatles, I just believe in me'. Were rich as kings, or at least culturally. Why do we need permission from outside? Our freedom? Can't we just take it?

- Well, I can't go home after all that's happened. You and I have something in common, rejection on both counts. We can live in a world of our own.

- Things are more mainstream now, even five years ago we couldn't hold hands in a mainstream bar, or out on the street. The line is drawn on kissing in public, but that time will come.

- Suppose that is the reason the local gay bar is out of business. People jacking off on the internet instead of socialising. It was not making money as a result.

- The local queens have to go somewhere, crisis or opportunity? You decide. Some of them will pick up where they left off.

- We shouldn't have to fight for all of this, private life is a human right. That and the right to be forgotten.

- I do wonder what goes on in that little head of yours, Cortina. I read books, watch television and play with my computer now and again. This is my lot in life. You're the only person who comes even close to understanding the real me. Not just about me being transgendered. You saw me as a person, and that's enough. With you, I can't deny that I am transgendered, transitioning, non-binary almost fully male. However, I still have ovaries and a uterus in case I need them.

- What does that mean, actually? That's plenty to get my head around.

- I was more than born in the wrong body, I was born in the wrong mind, wrong spirit.

- I suppose that is the way teenagers are now. They get worse with every generation. Remember *Jackie*? Holding hands isn't enough for today's adolescents, they have to do a weekend course on how to give a blow-job. I really do feel sorry for the youth of today, having to live up to these expectations. How to be cool, and all that. That's the worst job of all, second-guessing what your friends are up to, all that mind-reading. They know what buttons to press, especially with the

parents. Spare me!
- Don't like the sound of that.

- I don't either, but then, there's nothing I can do. Everything is so sexualised these days. Freud would have fun with that. Anyway, the park is fine, but I don't like those pigeons, rats with wings, as they're called. Ditto seagulls. They'd attack you if you're not careful.

- Pigeons do a very important job, Cortina. They clean up the gunk left by people that would otherwise be swept up by the dustmen. Everyone in this city has a part to play. The rule of this place is simple - don't bother anyone and no-one will bother you. Same goes for the winos in this place. You see plenty of them around here, thrown out by discerning wives who have had enough. Speaking of which, let's go home.

CHAPTER 14

Cortina kissed his hand and turned around. She was here for the long haul. The time was coming on, and she prayed that Philip would take her back to his home. They happily descended to the bottom of the stairs.

- No need for you to use crutches, I'll carry you.

- Careful, you'll do yourself an injury. Do you back in.

- Not to worry. The manual handling course stands me in good stead.

As he carried her up the stairs, seemingly without effort, she plunged her mouth against his, the ghost of junk food still on his mouth, the moment broken only by Philip rummaging for his keys, but that didn't matter.

He laid her down on the bed making space among the myriad of books scattered around. This was the shining light in the morning of their mutual souls. It was rapidly transcending into a higher realm, the avenues of pleasure, the peaks and valleys of desire that they could not but run away with.

- Can't really do much in the bedroom department, my apologies, but I can use my imagination. The biggest sexual organ is the brain, so that is where the fun starts. The fact that you are so well-read is a turn-on in itself.

- Not to worry. Please keep going, keep going.

- Cortina had indeed chosen the better part, in her vibrant imagination, and it was not to be taken from her. There was nothing to stop her using it to guide her through the thick and deep forest of coupling.

- *Keep going, keep going.*

She reached her hand underneath his cagoule, the better to explore the forbidden territory of his body, reaching towards his still-ample breasts.
He took her hand away.

- *Don't.*

She politely withdrew, much to her own chagrin, but with an understanding of the situation. She draped her arms over his shoulders, slowly welcoming his body, and it's trespass on hers.
He determinedly reached under her jumper, unhorsing her defences with one fell swoop. He removed her bra with ease that belied her initial reserve. But not to worry. He suckled her cockles through her still-nascent breasts.

Cortina slid her hands down his jeans, curious as to assess the situation and still going wherever she meant to go on. She grappled with his thighs, wrenching his jeans and underwear of in one fell swoop. Only his socks remained, but who cares?
Nothing remained in the were a logical conclusion, as

Cortina's fingers navigated his dark furry secret, drenched in sweat and slick sex juice, as she herself was. Her hand moved in and out like a hacksaw, grinding, getting deeper with every thrust. Philip grappled with her similar machinery, offering her honour all too readily. In all her life of solitude, she had never experienced such pleasure, a colossal wave of intimacy that engulfed them both.

She laid back on the bed, exhausted but happy.

- This deserves a cigarette, don't you think? Go on, have one. Have you any of that wine or yours left? Or any crisps, come to think of it?

- He removed into the bedside table and grabbed a part-opened package of smokes.

- Take one! God knows you've earned it!

- At worst, this was a hurdle to be cleared. At best, take it to a whole new level. I was once told that after your first sexual experience with someone, you can't go back to just holding hands.

- I do believe that is true. We went on a total abstract plane!

- You never hear of a woman raping a woman. Why? It's too much work.

- Whatever about work, I need a shower to begin with.

Cortina scanned the flat with new eyes, as if getting a new pair of glasses for the first time. It didn't matter that the flat was a mess, now she was here for the long haul. For better or worse, here she was, in a situation she could barely understand, much less have experienced. But never mind, it was enjoyable. At least now she could join the rest of the human race and sport herself whenever.

Philip came out of the shower.

- Guess what!

- What?

- I shaved today for the first time ever! Finally, getting to where I want to go!

- You still need to get a handle on that, I noticed a few cuts on your face. It takes practice, mind.

- Well, I was reliably informed that a sharp blade won't cut you, a blunt one would.

- You're lucky you didn't cut your face to ribbons.

- Never mind, this is a cause to celebrate! Christening the bed and all that. There's an opera on in the municipal theatre, called *The Nightingale and the Rose.*

- Never been to an opera before, but I know

what I like. Do we have to dress up for that?

- No. Just be yourself and enjoy the show. Read the subtitles if you have to. God knows they don't ask for a lot these days, not even to bring your own binoculars.

- I remember reading the story at school. Oscar Wilde wrote it, I think.

- You've nailed it girl.

- Did you ever go to the opera festival in Bayreuth?

- Well out of my budget. The tickets sell out very quickly as well.

- And the Wexford Opera House, what about that?

- They do the lesser-known operas, fair play to them. Don't have the time or the money to trek out there.

- An English-language opera, who'd have thought it?

- Well in most cases there are subtitles in English. There is a refrain going through the show, I'll teach it to you.

- How does it go?

- Repeat after me: 'Sing Me One Last Song, I Shall Be Very Lonely When You Are Gone'.

Once he was sure she had the bar off by heart, they adjourned to the bed once more.

CHAPTER 15

The celebrations still came thick and fast

- There's a party on this weekend, wanna come?

- Not really sure, whatever about my hometown, where I could get the odd naggin under the table, but the off-licences here will take no prisoners. Could I even pass muster, being underage and all that?

- Wouldn't chance it, girl, but still, it's an unwritten rule that you bring drink to a party.

- They will spot me. I'm only fifteen and a bit, they won't serve me. I told you that!

- Look, give me the money and I'll sort you out.

- Here's €5, go and get a four-pack. Some of that Polish stuff will go down a treat but avoid the super- cheap stuff like the plague. That stuff rots your gut and is only associated with winos anyway.

Philip took his racket and put it on.

- I'll just keep my head down, all right? On balance, we'd best split a bottle of wine between the two of us.

- Are you a wine buff or wine bluff?

- Somewhere in between. I do appreciate good wine now and again.

- How about Merlot? I know you like Merlot.

- Keep drinking and nobody gets hurt. Ha Ha, or maybe they do. Of course, people get hurt. Let's just pace ourselves and everything will be fine.

They sauntered to the party on the ghost estate, the house in question being an end-of-terrace affair, condemned to be unfinished by the economic powers that were. So much for private initiative.

- They're squatting?

- Don't hold that against them. At this rate it's money for old rope as far as the government is concerned. They couldn't finish it off construction-wise, so that crowd did it for them by putting it to good use.

A girl with shocking pink hair answered the door.

- Welcome, lads, how are he?

- Hi, I'm Philip, and this is my girlfriend, Cortina. This is a nice gaff, considering it's on a ghost estate.

- Well, we didn't want to be another homeless

statistic, she said gaily. We are putting the house to good use. The government should be thanking us for making use of what they didn't want anymore. We had to take matters into our own hands. The only drawback is that there always has to be someone in the house at any given time, so the authorities don't throw our stuff out, and us to boot.

- Okay...

- This isn't emergency accommodation, the electricity is installed as well, thanks to us. Take the power back!

- What, like Rage Against the Machine?

- Good call, let's go in. Is that the White Stripes on the stereo? Sounds great...

The girl's mobile rang. She quickly bolted to the back garden, which was quiet.

- Sorry, that was my mother. Never misses a trick, she does.

- How'd she know about the party?

- You haven't lived until you see what my mother gets up to. Mother's instinct, I guess. I swear, if I ever have kids I would cut them a bit of slack and let them make their own mistakes, even if they are supposed to be tucked up in their beds at this time of night.

In the kitchen, there was a somewhat local celebrity. He was a dwarf, and perpetual spoiling for a fight, though challenging guys twice his height and half his age. He was called, fittingly, Elastobastard. No doubt he was a fighter, due to his viciousness and small stature he was also known as the Ungrown Soldier.

- He's freaky! Where did he come from?

- Well, for your information, son, I work in mixed martial arts, or cage fighting, as it was called before. Leprechaun fighting, if the truth be told, the Americans are pure suckers for that. Had to do something once they banned dwarf-tossing on the continent. Needed another source of income. I am also plumping to get into the Guinness Book of Records, as the world's smallest bodybuilder mixed martial arts. Sounds cool?

- Bang for buck, buck for bang.

- He's the atypical alpha male, overcompensating for his small stature.

- It almost sounds illegal.

- He used to play centre forward for Subbuteo back in the day.

- Psycho killer, *quest que ce.*

- Watch him! He's trained to kill!

- He's the original Pocket Rocket.

Philip stepped up to the plate.

- Ok, Elastobastard, show me what you're made of. Take a pop at me, go on, hit me with it!

No sooner had Philip challenged him then he was flat on his back on the kitchen floor. He wasn't in serious pain, just stunned.

- There's something to be said for taking on someone your own size. If you want to plump for a medal, try the Gay Olympics. Chances are you'll get a gold medal just for turning up. Your dampness means that is a foregone conclusion. What actually happened that you couldn't get into the regular Olympics?

- A spinal tap finished me, they found illegal drugs in my system, and plenty of them.

True to form, he started bopping around the place under the influence of the old MDMA, and still showing off his old MMA skills while he was at it, punching above his weight, sweating like a pig.

- You know, he said to Philip, I once fronted a hardcore punk band that was called, surprise, surprise, The Elastic Band. It had a near-hit single once, only it dated from the time when Pete Burns of Dead or Alive actually looked like a man. It's been rarely played since. But not to worry. I've written a few songs. My latest song was written on the back of a bus.

Everyone tittered.

- What's wrong with that, writing songs on the back of buses? Many of the best songs ever written were composed on the back of buses. The back of a bus is Eton for songwriting. Look at 'What's Another Year' by Johnny Logan, or George Michael's 'Careless Whisper'.

- This new song, what's it called?

- *New Hero Zero*. There are the obvious references to GG Allin, but without the scatological references. It's more like Jello Biafra, in that regard he didn't sell out.

- Strange, nobody would even think of beating you up on stage.

- They wouldn't dare.

- I actually saw Jello Biafra in concert a few years ago. He was giving out about the privatisation of the prisons in America, and it really struck a chord with me. I even came up on stage and gave him a quick peck on the cheek. He said and did everything right, right down to the crowd-surfing, surprised he got away with that in such a small space.

- *Give Me Convenience or give me Death*?

Reminds me or my student days. 'Let's Lynch the Landlord' was one of my favourite tracks while in college, summed up my living quarters to a tee.

- Could he not sing it for us while he's here?

- Elastobastard won't sing it on his own. He's embarrassed at having to sing it in restricted company. Plus, the backing band isn't here. Then there's the problem of noise pollution, not to mention all of us being kicked out. You do know that we're just squatting here. Time is not on our side.

- This is hardcore punk rock at it's finest. Wouldn't want my daughter following them, though.

- Strangely, it didn't bother him much that Mitch, his drummer and closest friend, decided to become a born-again Christian.

- And what is he? A born-again Satanist?

- Not really sure that he was a Satanist to begin with. He wears a Thor's hammer around his neck, you do the math. Once he was in Iceland, he proposed to build a temple to the old gods. Don't know if that materialised, so don't quote me on that.

- Well, if you are disaffected enough and find the right ideology, you can go anywhere.

- I know. Look at the examples throughout history. Hitler, perhaps, would have agreed.

- He had to go to where it was ok to be a freak, rock and roll, perhaps punk! Some of those employers do take the piss either their vertically challenged employees, like putting up high-rise shelves and such like.

- Does that worry him? That everyone sees you as the local joke?

- I'm not paranoid, just being realistic! There's not much to choose between the two.

Sometimes they wondered if he really was a paranoid schizophrenic, or just paranoid, full stop. At least now the delusions were with good reason, and it wasn't all in his head. He could just be an overgrown teenager, with a permanent axe to grind.

- What the hell happened to him anyway? Besides the mixed martial arts.

- It all started when his mother told him, that when the ice-cream van started blaring the music, that went to show they were out of ice-cream. He wasn't happy with that. Nowadays, whenever an ice-cream van drops by, he goes nuts and bolts.

- Does he make habit of doing this?

- Yes, most times he cries his eyes out, but as he keeps saying, he will avenge in person.

- Just wait until the following afternoon. You can crash here and watch crash and burn. Hang on a second, I can hear it now! Jesus Christ, what business has an ice-cream van doing at this time of night? Most kids around here are tucked up in their beds!

- Watch him.

There was a plaintive scream from next door that was unmistakable. Elastobastard wasted no time to bolt outside, oblivious to the fact that all eyes were fixed on him, to see what would happen next.

He finally caught up with the ice-cream van whose presence and music had tormented him. Not one to care how much of a fool he was making himself out to be; this was his nemesis. He was on the roof of the van, shouting what sounded like:

- Give me an ice-cream! Give me a fucking ice-cream!

The driver came to an abrupt halt, shunting Elastobastard onto the asphalt in front of him. He got out.

- What the fuck is wrong with you? Do you want to get yourself killed?

Elastobastard looked up, from his superficial injuries.

- Sorry, I just wanted an ice-cream.
- You go through all this trouble, scaring the shit out of me, just for an ice-cream? You're lucky I'm not calling the guards, now what do you want?

- Mint chocolate, please.

- All right, soon, that's €2, please and you still owe me for the wipers you hung on to.

Elastobastard gave him a crumpled fiver.

- Thanks. Keep the change.

One could only surmise he left the ice-cream van, feeling reborn and refreshed, enough to glance at the sign 'Mind that Child!!' as it sped past. The curse was finally lifted.

Next day, he was clothed and sitting in his right mind, as if exorcised, being atypically quiet. He wished to go with Philip and Cortina, but Philip rebuffed him tactfully.

- Look, sort yourself out, and then get back to us. You have a lot of social adjustment to do. Try therapy, it'll sort your anger management issues out. Failing that, plough your frustration into what you do best. The gym, perhaps?

- Yes, keep up the weightlifting and your mixed martial arts, that's what you're good at. Let us know how you get on with *The Guinness book of Records,* if not the Olympics. We'll keep an eye out for you, never fear.

And at that, they walked down the avenue and were gone.

CHAPTER 16

Cortina was accosted on the school corridor again, where she was wont to run at high speed during break time. It was the closest to physical exercise she had in school, besides running around after a basketball while the teacher chatted to the school basketball team and gabbled about how well her husband's deer farm was getting on. Someone called her out, it was Ms. Masterson, what did she want? She seemed to be the only teacher to have to have an interest in her personally, as opposed to scolding and nagging her at every turn. Masterson taught Geography and Maths, with a touch of Religion to boot, and she wasn't afraid to use it.

- I just want you to complete these surveys for me, it won't take long. Come with me to the Hospitality room and I'll show you.

What was this? Multiple-choice questionnaires, and the odd sliding-scale to boot. Interviews, more interviews, surveys. That would wreck anyone's head, but for now she didn't mind. She duly grabbed a pen and began to tick the various boxes.

- Take your time, there's no rush. It's still lunchtime, never fear.

She even gave her a Mars bar for her troubles.

- Thanks.

- Just so you should know, all this is in the strictest confidence.

- Thank you, Ms. Masterson.

Cortina surreptitiously glanced at her notes, the title declaring itself 'The Phenomenon of the Class Clown in Second-level Educational Institutions'.

- And another thing: keep a diary for me. Just to track your progress. I will get back to you soon.

Cortina took this in her stride. She could warm to this level of attention.

At one point she called up to the staff room on an unrelated matter, namely, to hand an overdue essay to Mr. Hanrahan, the Biology teacher.

- By the way, where's Ms. Masterson? I have a survey completed for her.

- She's teaching class 4A.

At that she approached the class of 4A and politely knocked on the door. As she crossed the threshold, the whole class tittered.
- Hi there Cortina, just entertaining the troops with your diary.

What? How could she do this? Stripping her naked in

front of everyone.

- I thought that this diary was in the strictest confidence?

- Couldn't help it, it was too funny to pass up. You're quite the gifted writer! It's got to the stage where I don't even have to open the diary up, it's the same story every time.

- As long as none of you can take credit for what is mine... I'll be a straight A student all right, but not at your say-so, or have you breathing down my neck.

Cortina quickly bolted out the door. Whatever about confidence, her confidence in herself, Ms. Masterson, her friends and everything else was shattered. She turned to the Geography room, which was vacant for once, and sat down and wept. She always wept in private, no matter how public her grief was.
Once her eyes had finally wept their gratuitous portions of tears, she eyed the room, and spotted the DVD player.

- If you can't join them, beat them.

She shoved it into her bag. She knew that her cards were marked from the very beginning, one more antic wouldn't make much of a difference. The system was wasted on her. There was such a thing as the right to be forgotten. Ashes to ashes, dust to dust. Misrepresented, misplace, mistaken, misbegotten. The singular music of the stars.

- Looked how she turned on me. To my

disadvantage, no doubt. Does the phrase 'professional distance' mean anything to her? I don't owe her an explanation for my actions. I am under constant surveillance and she didn't even have the manners to tell me? Talk about channels of information. She's straining out gnats and swallowing camels.

That was nothing compared to what happened that Saturday in the Shamrock. It was called the Pub from the Moon, by her friends who were old enough to drink, because there was absolutely no atmosphere there whatsoever, apart from the ubiquitous drunk arguing with himself in the far corner. Funnily enough, she was always warned to avoid that place, because of something called Wife-beaters brew. The fact that Dad had no wife to beat seemed to be irrelevant, he drank there anyway, but it seemed odd that the other punters went there every night just to have conversations with themselves, or the aforementioned drunk who was supported solely by the barstool and his own tawdry ambitions.

Cortina alighted into the bar to use the toilet, enough to see her Dad and Marie in the far corner.

- Hello, Cortina, what brings you here?

- Using the toilets. What's your excuse? More to the point, what are you doing with my dad?

- We just got engaged.

- Mother of Jesus, no!

- Yes, actually, said Marie with a trademark smirk.

- I know you hooked up with someone, but this..!

- It had to come out sometime. Aren't you happy for us?

- We were alright as we were, Dad, why complicate matters? When did this start?

- We met at the PTA meeting six months ago and took it from there.

- Your father is a very nice man, intoned Marie, injecting just the right amount of sarcasm. She put her hand on Dad's shoulder. The three of us will be very happy together. Isn't that right, Cortina?

- Over my dead body.

- And another thing, I have another survey sheet you might want to look at, first thing Monday!

It was proper, for Cortina, under the circumstances, to be angry.

- So, you two know each other? Inquired Dad, who in his jubilation conveniently disguised the fact that they did indeed know each other.

- Yes, Dad, she teaches me at school, as if you didn't know. I still don't know why my actions are the stuff of legend if they were just attention-seeking and nothing more. What's so glamorous about being a snitch, anyway? It's not studying or research, it's obsession.

- As I was saying...

- If you have something to tell him, tell him. Makes no difference to me at this stage.

- But it doesn't have to be like this. We can be such pals!

- Shove your dove, Marie.

- Why do you go out of your way to draw the wrong kind of attention to yourself?

It seemed, at that point, that abortion of a mother figure by the child was not such an outlandish idea after all. Failing that, the step-parent and child should easily get divorced. Suicide crossed her mind, but she knew life hadn't finished with her yet. She fulfilled her original mission of using the toilets. Marie was waiting outside.

- Cheeky fucker. I'll put some manners on you. You're in trouble up to your neck.

Dad was a bit nonplussed but knew what was going on.

- What are you doing here, anyway? You're a little young to be drinking. Get out.

170

- I'm a professional, I can do what I like.

- Professional what, exactly? Troublemaker, dosser? said Marie, it's good that you're still here. We've something to show you.

Cortina sat down, centering herself around a sparkling solitaire diamond ring placed on Marie's finger.

- That's exactly what I want. An engagement ring worth €5000.

- What? Are you crazy? That would nearly pay for the reception! Not to mention my college fees.

- Look at it as an investment, on a domestic level. Once Marie is settled in, we'll all be happy.

- I suppose you were regaling him with tales of my misdeeds?

- We'll talk about that later. Aren't you going to congratulate us?

- Er...

- Let's raise a toast.
At that Cortina perfunctorily raised a glass and bolted out the door.

Upon arriving home, it now seemed four cans for a fiver

never seemed so sweet. The fact that she looked slightly older was a distinct advantage when she alighted into the off-licence on several occasions. She was unhappy in her new situation, sinking her illicit drinks in front of the television. She stayed up long enough to witness Dad's key being twisted in the lock.

- Don't you see, Cortina, that I am still bereft since your mother died?

- Dad, it's not a question of substituting one female role model for another, especially another mother. She certainly doesn't fit the bill.

- You're a big girl now, leave us alone. It was never my intention to fall in love, it just happened.

- Whatever happened to the confidentiality clause.

- I do have a right to know. I am paying for your education. You have the right to remain silent, until further notice. Your situation is almost a self-fulfilling prophecy. Even if she is stepping into your mother's shoes, she wouldn't want to be your sister. But it's only for your own good! She actually cares about you!

- I'm not going to stand around listening to this, said Cortina.

At that, she turned on her heel, and was gone.

CHAPTER 17

After much research, Hiram found Cortina. It was outside the city library, and the pickings, he surmised, would be rich. So much for an educated meeting on the street. He gently accosted her on the way in.

- Cortina! Please come home! This is an emergency!

- No! Not while she's there!

She bolted from Hiram's grasp and sprinted free. He called out to her in a booming voice, not caring who was listening.

- You don't have to worry about Marie, she's dead!

Cortina turned around in shock.

- Dead? How did this happen?

- Come to the car and I will tell you.

They marched purposefully towards the multi-storey carpark, there being a thick silence as they got in the car.

- Jesus, how did that happen? With Marie?

- Just got up one morning and collapsed. The post-mortem said she had a brain aneurysm. The coroner safely ruled out foul play. But I can say with all honesty that you didn't help the poor creature.

- Well, it's no sin to take her out of circulation. Death by misadventure. Some misadventure. She definitely put me to shame, karma catching up with her. Ace.

- Not only her, but your dad is in hospital, fighting for his life. We're talking intensive care!

- What's wrong with him?

- Garda Dunne and his pals beat him up.

- What was that about?

- Well, whatever the guards did him for, it wasn't for car tax and insurance. Apparently, Marie was fucking Garda Dunne on the sky, and after she died, those bastards gave him the biggest kicking he ever experienced, calling him a 'murdering bastard', and knocking the sugar out of him.

- Please don't let him die! Is he okay? Please, God!

She grabbed the Padre Pio motorist's prayer and the rosary beads hanging from the rearview and prayed fervently.

- Your father has lost the two most important women in his life, and nearly lost his life while he was at it, hanging by a thread. Of course, he's distraught.

- Well, I suppose thirty years old like Marie don't just die of natural causes. As they say, if you die with a mortal sin on your soul you will go to hell.

- You have Marie's death on your conscience, never fear. By the way, what are you doing with a Magic Tree air freshener in your hand? Forest Fresh never saved anyone's life.

- I know what the rosary is for. You took your time to find me, if you were that desperate.

- We thought you'd come home once the money from the nest-egg had gone. Anyway, we had to find you once Marie died, even if it was for you to spit on her grave. Furthermore, you father needs you. Parishes are splendid rumour mills; everyone knew about Marie's death almost before he did. Anyway, how about *you*? This is a matter of urgency, Cortina, he might not last the distance.

- Some turnaround that was. Finally got his priorities in order. I hope Marie thought so.

- You're not the only one with problems,

Cortina, I have too. One person whom I took in robbed us blind overnight. Took everything that wasn't nailed down or couldn't be carried.

- You had that coming. Eilís was proved right in the end. What did you expect?

- I'm not worried about the money, there are some things that can't be replaced, like wedding presents, or my mother-in-law's jewellery.

- Sentimental value?

- Yes, I was waiting for that. Though I would have liked for my valuables to be brought back in one piece, if the guards can recover them.

- Anyway, about Dad. This is the worst case of Schrödinger's cat that has ever existed. Is he dead? Is he alive?

- He was thinking the same about you. Not a squeak for so long, wherever you were. Anyway, this is down to Ockham's razor, the simplest explanation is most probably the correct one. Know you couldn't resist libraries, so I scouted for you there.

They rushed themselves into the hospital. Cortina was barely able to keep up with Hiram as he skimmed past the orderlies, doctors, porters and various particulars as he sauntered with intent, deftly turning the corner into the intensive care ward. He pressed the buzzer and waited briefly.

- Hello, this is Hiram Richards and Cortina, Ger Murray's daughter. I'll wait outside, give the two of you some privacy.

She turned the corner and descended on the corner bed. She initially didn't recognize him, being bruised, bloodied, encased in various casts and bandages. Not to mention the various machines he was hooked up to. She quietly sat herself down at his bedside.

- Dad? It's me, Cortina. No, you're not hallucinating, it's me. Don't cry, I'm here now, and I am here for good. It's just you and me now.

He rolled his eyes in shock.

- Cortina! Thank God you're here. God knows I missed you.

- Whatever went on, I'm sorry.

- And here's me thinking you ran off to join Isis or something! Very big adventure! How did you get by?

- Means and ways. Sharp wit and blunt instruments. Can you forgive me?

Cortina took her father's hand and squeezed it, observing the sutures of worry and neglect on his face. His iron grey hair had diminished to a fine white and he had grown a whisper of a beard he was too weak to shave. He squeezed back, as if he never wanted to let her go. The shallowness of breath had gone, replaced by an incessant wave of deep sighs, his eyes opening, fixed on his daughter. He made an attempt to sit up but was more than happy to let Cortina prop up on the cushions supporting the upper half of his body.

- My princess! he gasped, let me see you!

- I am sorry for your trouble, and the trouble I caused you. Don't die on me, please!

- Well, whatever else, I have learned never to trust a woman with my heart, no matter who she is.

- Don't talk like that, Dad, come on, sit up.

- What did you get up to, or dare I ask?

- This and that. I've had a few scrapes myself. I know Marie had the guts to ruin people's lives. What happened to her?

- Just woke up and collapsed. Cerebral aneurysm, would have happened anyway.

- Talk about serendipity.

- You were conspicuous by your absence at her funeral. Everyone was asking questions about you. One coupon short of a toaster you were,

I had to explain the situation to everyone.

- My hands and nose are clean. How arrogant can you get, thinking she can plug a mother-shaped gaping hole my psyche? Serves her right.

- You put too much pressure on her. That finished her off more than anything.

- I know you hate hospitals. You always said, 'Good to have them but bad to need them'. What about Garda Dunne? What did he do to you?

- Well, the local Garda unit, comprising of Dunne and his mates, pulled me over in their unmarked Garda car, took me out and knocked seven shades of sugar out of me, calling me a 'murdering bastard', all because Marie died in my house. It was the I learned he was having an affair with her. I don't know which was worse, the physical or mental bruising, or even you, not being there when I needed you.

- You didn't deserve any of this. Are you pressing charges?

- What sort of planet are you on, girl? I'm not in a position to press charges. Dunne is still giving winning tips on horses; I am reliably informed. His crowd are nearly above the law, even if their job is to enforce it. I'm off the record, understand?

- Hmmm...

- I think I deserve a better explanation for your actions than that. If you're going to be vague, at least be coherently vague.

- Why is it everyone's business what I experienced in my life? Why do you think I bolted?

- You're headstrong, girl, but you're also underage. Of course, it's everyone's business. I know you have a right to privacy, but it's only for your own good. Wait until you pass the Rubicon of eighteen, then you can do what you like.

- Sorry if I cramp your style, putting you through all this trouble.

- Not a question of style. People came for you, looking for you. I didn't deserve this, having to choose between a wife and a child. You're still a child in lots of ways, Cortina, you still can't face things alone, the truth will always find a way. I was even prepared to meet you in heaven, at one point.

- My situation was like Virginia Woolf's essay, 'A Room of One's Own'. I needed space and plenty of it. Anyway, we're doing a perfectly good job, in the here and now. Just the two of us, picture that? That's all we need.

- Don't want you to die unfulfilled, like your mother, or me, for that matter. You're well able to fight your corner, and you've matured a lot in the past while. And you're smoking again! You're worse than Eilís with her Huff and Puff episodes. Just wondering if you were taking the wrong things, like cannabis, ecstasy, heroin, suchlike.

- Nothing for you to worry about. I'm still here, and the picture of health. No track marks up my arm, or sleeping rough, for that matter.

- You'll have to make your own mistakes in this life, that is how you'll learn. I made some bad choices in my life. After a few weeks, the pain doesn't get any worse.

- Don't die on me, please!

- Young devil, old Saint. Or is it the other day round? Like Nano Nagle, a tearaway while young, but then became a saint. Venerable, so to speak.

- Don't let anyone come between us again! Time, distance, speed, you name it.

- I just hope you were wiser because of the event. It's easy to be wise after the event. You've learned a hard lesson, girl. In some cultures, you would get your head chopped off. That and fifty lashes for your trouble.

- I've seen a bit of the world and I must conclude that I'm not really ready for it yet. But you said as much just now, these things are sent to test us.

- Just promise you will never do that again. I don't care how much you hurt me, or what happened, I am still your father, and I'm still proud of you. I know you got expelled on purpose, Cortina. We have to have a serious talk about your education, you know, your schooling. But that's a story for another day.

CHAPTER 18

Cortina turned to Hiram in the corridor, who was watching from a distance. He tactfully kept his distance, even if the look on his face indicated that he was looking for news, or about to give an opinion.

- You can't choose who you fall in love with, not even your dad. You'll be an orphan by the time he's finished with you. Who'll look after you then?

- Well, I have demonstrated, beyond a reasonable doubt, that I am well able to take care of myself. By the way, I have to ring Philip, leave a message for him.

- Who's Philip?

- The best guy in the world. He has to know what's going on.

- There are various sordid goings on in that part of the world that you wouldn't understand, even after what you have experienced.

- For what exactly?

- Just for company, among other things. So, I see. But you can't get anywhere without qualifications, even if it is just the Leaving Cert.

185

You want to go to college, right? The way you are, you are rotting on the vine. We have to go now. You can stay at my place until further notice. You might be headstrong, but you still need looking after.

- Not to worry, times nearly up. Will talk to you tomorrow.

CHAPTER 19

Hiram and Cortina approached the car park. The wounds were still raw on everyone's part, and picking away at these was at best, pointless. So, they both kept their traps shut, as they did when approaching his house.

As they approached the kitchen door, they were greeted by the children, all falling over themselves to give her a hero's welcome. Eilís, for all that was more circumspect, scouting for developments, at least, that which was written all over her face.

Hiram purposely accosted Eilís on the back doorstep.

- Look, Eilís, she's been through enough today, so no interrogation please.

Eilís fixed her gaze on her, as is to guage what sorry mystery had descended on her doorstep this time, only this time, she knew this season's miscreant.

- Well then, to whom do we owe the pleasure?

Cortina was summarily silent.

- You could at least apologise to your father for putting him through this! He's at your mercy and you at his.

Eilís descended into the living room, followed by Hiram, leaving Cortina alone in the kitchen. It was obvious that

they needed a private word together. Let them.
- How'd you find her, anyway?

- Caught her outside the city library this morning. But that's not important, she's here now, safe and sound, that's all that matters. I know the local library is closed on Mondays, couldn't patrol all the second-hand bookstores and cafés around the place. Safe bet getting there first thing on Tuesday. It was either that or stalking every second-hand bookshop in town and I couldn't pull that one off on a logistical level. It would burn me out.

Cortina was quick to respond to the conversation, if only to put Eilís in her place.

- Heard about you getting robbed, by the way. Yes, I am sorry to hear that.

- Yes, it had to happen at some stage. I always told him to set up an orphanage or a drying-out hostel outside his own dwelling, but oh no, had to operate from his own gaff. And now look what happened - everything gone that wasn't nailed down. Wedding presents, crockery, cutlery, and that American mantelpiece clock which belonged to my grandmother, that was priceless, no chance of getting that back ever! And there was no insurance payout because we let her into the house. Asking for it, so they say.

- Who was this person, anyway?

- Some junkie off the street. You do the math. Stole everything here to feed his habit.

- Sorry to hear that, as I said.

- Anyway, your timing was impeccable, to say nothing of Hiram. Another few days and your dad would have kicked the bucket. You'd have been the world's oldest orphan.

- Am I now to be blamed for everything?

- Give an inch of Christian compassion, and they'll take a mile to perdition. Isn't that right, Hiram? Hmmm?

- That's enough, Eilís. Less of your sarcasm. I've reconciled the two, and Ger is on the mend.

- Well, the kids are looking for news on your various adventures, said Eilís.

- Where did you go, Cortina? What happened? What did you do?

- Don't bombard her with so many questions, it's very rude. Dinner is nearly ready anyway. We can talk then.

- I'll tell you after dinner, lads, never fear.

- Certainly an adventure, if nothing else, surmised Eilís. What were you up to? I'd really like to know.

- I know there were various rumors about her in her absence around the country and even internationally. Sightings everywhere except where you actually were! London, Cardiff, Dublin. They had to check all these leads, even if they knew they were only wasting their time. But there was no urgency; we surmised that once the money was gone you would come home.

- I understand why you intercepted me outside the library, with dad being the way he is. What was the worst thing I could possibly have done?

- Sex and drugs and rock and roll, perhaps?

- And if I were, so what?

- There was no way the shit would not have hit the fan. Of course, people are going to look for you! Of course, you were more conspicuous by your absence!

- Why is my life so fascinating to people all of a sudden? I was myself once, now I'm a cliché. Rebellious teenager strikes again.

- We were entertained, flummoxed, even slightly pissed off, but never bored. Even if we were hoping on the back of false testimonials.

- Everyone is talking about me.

- You know Oscar Wilde's quip on that. Don't

190

flatter yourself, there's other things going on in this town besides you.
- Such as?

- There's been a recent spate of burglaries around here, including the scrapyard.

- Fuck me! *What?*

- Apparently there was a huge traveller wedding in town recently, everything had to shut down. Probably adjourning from Cahirmee horse fair. You should see the size of some of those events, they don't come cheap. I mean there has to be some means of paying for them, fair means or foul. Ergo the burglaries. And the worst thing was your father was totally oblivious to this, convalescing in hospital. Let's make sure that for the moment he stays oblivious to all this for now while he recovers. Least said, soonest mended. Not a word to him about that, ok?

- It's hardly the silly season, you'd think that everyone had nothing better to do than look for you. How did you survive? Begging? Rich benefactor?

- That's none of your business. Speaking of benefactors, I have to ring Philip.

- Who's Philip?

- The best guy in the world.

- Ah, a boyfriend in the making. Can't be bad!

- Can't reach him, though.

- If you keep ringing him, it'll freak him out, and you won't see him for dust. Give him a break, play hard to get.

- That's an insult to injury.

- It is my business; I beg your pardon. You were three months away without leave and your father sick with worry. Of course, it's my business, I am family! said Hiram.

- I don't mind you coming here, Cortina. On the contrary, I enjoy having our little discussions about things, personal stuff as well, although that's off the record. But I'd really like to know what you got up there! Eilís could not contain her curiousity.

Hiram quickly got up from the dinner table.

- Go to bed, all of you. Every day has enough grief of its own. We'll talk about things in the morning.

192

CHAPTER 20

The following morning brought its own comforts, and the relative luxury was not lost on Cortina, as she tucked in to Eilís' immaculate breakfast. Daytime television never seemed so sweet, especially over a bowl of cornflakes and the perfect cup of orange and a decent cup of real coffee. Whatever one would say about nurses being unskilled workers, the level of care Dad was given was second to none. He was certainly in safe hands.

Cortina glanced at her watch. It was 11am.

- Hiram! Let's go to the hospital!

- Fair enough. Go to see him.

- I suppose travel broadens the mind, don't you think, Hiram? said Eilís sarcastically.

- OK, Eilís, that's enough, said Hiram, you're not the only one with problems. And your sarcasm is wearing thin regarding everyone here.

Eilís now knew well enough to leave well alone, but her inquisitiveness got the better of her.

- Thought you would come home pretty sharpish once the money from the wedding fund would run out. Although in fairness, €400 isn't going to last you very long in the real world. How did you get

by on that?
- Went to McLaughlin's solicitors in a compensation case after I fell in a pothole.

Hiram had to laugh.

- McLaughlin's the alcoholic ambulance-chaser? I went to college with him. A dubious sort, so he was always in for a cheap buck. Always in the early morning pub and never thought of anything past his next drop of whiskey. Lazy fucker.

- I didn't get any compensation, but I did meet Philip. He lived next door to him. He was the best sweetheart there was.

- I knew another solicitor who came to a bad end; he eked out a living as a singing telegram. He got more money by soliciting than by being a solicitor. Don't know how, but he was happier that way. So, on that instance, let's go! Dad's waiting!

Cortina and Hiram buzzed into the intensive care ward, only to find that Dad was moved to a regular ward. They were given a barrage of instructions as to how to get there.

The nurse greeted them.

- That father of yours is not well when he came in. He was refusing food, rambling incessantly about his Ford Cortina. Why he's obsessing over a car in his condition I'll never know. Although I do

194

know that some blokes love their cars above their wives and families, especially if it's a model that's been obsolete for quite some time.

- No, he means me. I'm Ford Cortina, his daughter. I was named after the car. So there.

- I already see a significant improvement in him, with his daughter near him, that was better than any drug we can prescribe. He should keep taking them, whatever they are! You are a mechanic's daughter? You fix people like your old man fixes cars.

- I have fixed the odd car myself. Pushed them safely off the road when the battery died, although I drew the line at using jump leads. I wasn't allowed to use them. But he'll be fine, will he?

Another nurse cut in.

- You're Ger Murray's daughter, aren't you? I must say a have never seen someone improve so quickly as him! Whatever you've got, sell it on the open market! You'll make a fortune!

Dad was seated on the easy chair, reading a tattered magazine.

- Dad, it's me, Cortina.

She leaned over his forehead and gave him a kiss.

- Is the shock too much for you?

- Not at all, he said in a forced whisper, where were you?

- Back at Hiram's. But that's not important, we have to look after you now.

He rolled his eyes in her general direction.

- Please dear, don't ever trust a Garda from now on. I know they are supposed to be guardians of the peace, but at best they let you down, at worst they steal your girlfriend and at ultimate worst they pulverise you to within an inch of your life.

- Point taken, dad. Take it you won't be servicing his white Ford Mondeo anytime soon.

- It's good that you're here.

- How are you? I've dug up your old vinyl collection good to see vinyl is making a comeback, as they say, if you keep something for long enough it will come back into fashion. I'm pretty sure cassettes are not too far behind. Give or take another fifteen years.

- If you say so.

- I brought the record player as well. How about we throw on some of your Moe Tucker albums?

- As in The Velvet Underground?

- Great. Which one? *I Spent A Week There the Other Night* or *Life in Exile After Abdication*?

- Either.

It was great to sense the satisfaction that populated the room, the sound of 'That's B.A.D' seeping from the speakers.

- Turn on the television, Cortina, is *The X Factor* on? I know you like watching that.

- So, what about *The X Factor*? So, what if they can sing? Loads of people can bloody sing. Come down to the Shamrock on a Friday night for a karaoke if you don't believe me. You know that better than anyone.

- I must say that I felt a little sorry for Glen Matlock when he got booted out of the Sex Pistols. But it's not cool to admit that in public.

- The dinner trolley should be here by now. Have some dinner, Dad. Keep your strength up. I'll call around with a large bottle of Lucozade next time I'm here.

- Those fuckers nearly killed me, thirteen fractured ribs, two broken arms, one punctured lung, being punched and kicked into oblivion.

She took his hand.

197

- God you're very cold.

She breathed onto his hand to warm him up. He took a deep breath himself, as if to declare something.

- Whatever about me, we must talk about you, your education and health is more important than any scrapyard. That is why I enrolled you in boarding school at Pres. The independent life suits you; I gather. Knock off a few of your sharp edges. Moved heaven and earth to find a place for you and I was lucky! You should appreciate that.

- But why?

- You want to go to college, right? You can't get anywhere without qualifications, even if it is just the Leaving Cert.

- Dad, what now?

- It was also mooted by Marie that you see a psychiatrist, after your attack on the apprentice episode, but initially I was dead against it before all this happened. There was a twelve-week waiting list, but now your time has come. We finally have an appointment for you and Dr Broderick.

- What?

- You're far too intelligent for lolling around in a scrapyard, Cortina. I want the best for you, and I really want to make you succeed in life. The scrapyard isn't even open now, since I got beaten up. No one comes there, unless it's the travelers, I believe.

- You could at least have consulted me, you know, about the psychiatrist, before I went away.

- You weren't there to consult, gallivanting as you were. Your poor father worrying about you, and that bitch not even pretending to care.

- I don't owe an explanation to anyone!

- Yes, however about those, I'm more concerned about you and your future, as opposed to your past.

Cortina surrendered.

- No student is above his master, I guess. It is enough for the student to be like the master. You're right. I do need a bit of discipline. Hate being at a loose end.

- Family is the most important thing in this life, Cortina.

- I agree, even if some slapper almost tore it apart.

- Like that song by the Seekers, 'You Wouldn't Find Another Fool Like Me'. But I never gave up on you. I held out till the very bitter end. And so did you.

- I'm going home. That's enough over-analysis for

one day. Change the record.

- Like what? What about The Rolling Stones?

- Whatever. Do you want the Rolling Stones in the seventies or the Rolling Stones in their seventies?

- Throw on *Voodoo Lounge* and we'll discuss our options afterwards.

CHAPTER 21

Hiram accompanied Cortina to Pearses Park Hospital, where her appointment with Dr Broderick was to be held.

- Fuck me. Pearse's Park Psychiatric Hospital. Same hospital, my mother was in after giving birth!

Hiram was reserved, silent and unflummoxed as he turned the corner into the hospital grounds. There were immaculately manicured lawns through a number of decrepit self-contained units up steep hills, and everywhere the units were painted a predictable shade of magnolia and terracotta. Cortina took a break from her self-pity to observe the hospital grounds.

- There's a pitch and putt course here. What's the attraction of them to these places?

- Not exclusively for golfers, mind you. Or pitch and putt enthusiasts. This was a TB hospital to begin with. It had to be bright and airy, so the patients would recover rather quickly.

The two descended into the reception area and waited their turn. The kindly lady told them that Dr Broderick would see them in a minute or so.

- Now be good and tell him *everything*. All that happened to you in recent memory, and don't skimp on the details! It's for your own good, trust me.

- Fine.

- And don't say anything to the fellow patients.

- I know the drill.

- Good. You're on the right track already.

- Tell me, Hiram, is this a punishment for absconding?

- It's more of a quarantine situation, like the Apollo 11 moon astronauts landed on re-entry to earth from the moon, crash-landing in the Pacific before they could re-enter civilised society. It worked too, mind. It's a preventative measure, the likelihood of psychosis and all that. Also had to treat your mother for that way back when. Broderick will sort you out, never fear. He's been in the business for years.

A kindly lady ushered her in. Cortina could not but bless herself on the way in.
Once she was in, send observed that Broderick was a stocky fellow who had a broken leg in a large cast and a whiff of seniority about him. He took one look at Cortina, scanning her top to toe and he knew he was in for the kill.

- Come in, he declared, take a seat.

Cortina did as she was told.

- Right then, he declared, what have you to say for yourself?

- I had problems with my dad's fiancée and I bolted. Can't say fairer than that.

- Is that it? Is that what you've coming to tell me about?

- In a nutshell, yes.

- And you were a tearaway at school, I gather.

- That's about the size of it.

- I heard you got expelled from school for stealing a DVD player.

- That's as good as it gets.

- And you ran away from home?

- It had to be done.

- Did you ever come across the phrase, 'faraway hills are green?'

- Yes.

- What does it mean? Or 'People who live in glass houses shouldn't throw stones'.

- Why are you throwing clichés at me? My whole

life is a war against cliché.

- And you did that by doing a runner? Charming, that's grounds for you to be taken into care. No wonder your father's looking a bit ragged.

- I felt sorry for him but not much. He's only as good as the woman he hooked up with. I took a road trip over persistent paranoia. You know where I'm coming from. And you're the last person I would come to with my problems. Anyone who comes to a psychiatrist should have his head examined. Am I to go the same way as my mother?

- It would be against her wishes if she were alive, but you are definitely following her footsteps.

- What is this about my mother?

- I am not at liberty to discuss your mother's situation with you. She's dead and gone.

- Not even my dad? He is still recuperating in hospital.

- That he is. No thanks to you. What'd you get up to anyway? Drugs? Drink? Sex? Rock and roll? Or all four?

- None of your fucking business.

- We'll find out fairly soon, mark my words.

- Suppose I just tell you that I am a citizen of the

whole world.
- You are taking the piss?

- No, taking my cue from Socrates. I crave freedom, and flexibility at that. Anyway I'm not suicidal, so perish the thought in your situation. I still don't regret my actions, so there. Can you not just accept me as I am? Everyone in your position is fucking retarded.

- We don't use the word 'retarded' anymore. What we say is 'special needs'.

- What is so special about *your* needs? Who cares? You broke your leg, so what?

- Never mind my needs, we are here to see to yours.

- How can anyone possibly know how I feel?

- Is that right? Well, judging on what you told me, there's a bed in this hospital waiting for you! I made the relevant phone call before you even got past the front door!

- Well, I'm sorry but I am going nowhere.

- What do you want from me?

- I want to go home to my dad.

Broderick let out a callous laugh.

- Funny that, he wasn't good enough for you when

205

you bolted all that time ago. You're right up there with those teenage girls who went to join Isis.

- Not my field of expertise, terrorism. Am too much of a pacifist for that.

- Your command is not my wish, girl, there are certain procedures in place for dealing with the likes of you. In other words, your ass is mine. If you don't cop yourself on, you'll be sectioned.

- Sectioned? What the hell is that?

- Locked up for the foreseeable future.

- No fucking way, sugar.

- Yes way, sugar. There's a bed here, waiting for you, get used to it!

- Why am I here, why are you here? I suppose you were banging Marie on the sly as well, up there with Garda Dunne. My situation here seems more like payment for services rendered, in other words. She would say that, wouldn't she? There's no way I am staying here!

At that she shunted herself out, but Dr Broderick followed her with intent. Hiram took one look at her and knew the situation was dire.

- Bloody hell, did I just overplay my hand, Hiram? Said too much?

- So, what is the story? When it comes to specialists, there's no such thing as too much information, said Hiram.

Broderick positioned himself in the doorway, on crutches.

- We're keeping her in for the next while, they have a bed for her in here.

- I don't want to go, Hiram, please don't tell dad about this, it'll kill him.

- He has a right to know, he is your legal guardian, for all that, even if he is convalescing. Just grab a set of pyjamas, some toiletries, a change of clothes and a towel and let's go. This is for your own benefit, I don't want to see you in here either, any more than your father does.

- At the very least we'll teach you a bit of manners, snarled Broderick.

- What about that the report that Marie was so fond of? Where's that going to go?

- That's not important right now. Get yourself sorted and we'll discuss your options afterwards, said Hiram.

- There's something to be said for someone who knows me better than I do myself. These fucking so-called experts, psychiatrists. Breaking up homes, splitting up couples, doing more harm than good.

- This is almost a self-fulfilling prophecy, with you, said Broderick, see you sharpish.

CHAPTER 22

Cortina knew already that the ultimate function of these institutions was dumping grounds for costly maiden aunts, a short sharp shock for recidivist daughters, like herself, or wives disposed by errant husbands, so they could sport themselves while they could with their pretty new mistresses. She never thought in a million years that she could fit at least one criterion for these, but there you go.

Hiram, for his part, gave her some sage advice. Again.

- Give the minimum of information about yourself to anyone apart from the doctors. Keep your head down and say nothing, either to those inside or out. You've enough of a cross to bear anyway. Drug users, schizophrenics, parasuicides, borderlines, bipolar, they're all there. Plus, those that are there all their lives and are institutionalised plaintively looking for that elusive cigarette. In that case, just give them a cigarette and send them on their way. But the latter doesn't concern you. The days of incarceration for life are long gone, they want to see you back on your feet in no time, and home with the minimum of fuss.

At that he proffered her a few packets of cigarettes.

- I brought you these. You might as well take them; they are hard currency in there. Got these against my better judgement, but you're going to need someone on your side. This is not primary school, it's fine to buy your friends in here.

- Once again I have been dominated by retards. First school, now this.

- Don't get smart. Well, this place was built for tuberculosis patients to begin with, as I said. It was a taboo subject the same as mental illness is now.

- I don't suffer from insanity, Hiram, in fact I quite enjoy it. The voices in my head actually entertain me, I'm never bored, in fact, and I have a high boredom threshold. Why should I be the one to be incarcerated? I just do things slightly differently.

- You can't judge yourself against others, you don't know what they are going through and with any luck, they won't know your situation either.

- After seeing that, I am fully convinced that it is not me, the system is out of order. Leave me alone, Hiram, I have to sort myself out.

- Okay, let the medical crew do their job. They'll show you around.

- I have to change into my night clothes, it's standard practice here, until further notice. Talk to you soon.

- Fine. Talk to you soon. Talk to you tomorrow.

\- Make sure Dad is fine, will you?

\- Of course I will, said Hiram, he gave her a hug and went on his way.

CHAPTER 23

One of the nurses accosted Cortina and combed through her belongings, before instructing her to change into night clothes. Once she was in this uniform, she was left alone. She went outside, regaled in her fluffy nightgown, with the realisation that she had mislaid her cigarettes. She turned to the girl beside her in the hope she had a cigarette to spare.

As luck would have it, someone proffered a cigarette to Cortina before she had the audacity to ask.

- Hey, what's your name?

- I'll tell you. But please don't laugh.

- Couldn't be much worse than mine. Go ahead.

- Richareta. Yours?

- Ford Cortina. Don't make a joke about this, that is my actual name. Even if it is after a car.

At that she reminisced on Broderick's question: *People who live in glass houses shouldn't throw stones.* Especially when it came to your parents' choice of name for their offspring.

- How'd you end up with a name like that? Being named after a car?

- Something to do with offering your firstborn to

213

the gods of vehicular technology. What's your excuse?

- Named after my father. Salt of the earth. The mother nagged him to death. Should face criminal charges, but apparently nagging is not classed as an offensive weapon in the courts. The less I see of her, the happier I'll be. Ditto her second husband. Narcissists, the both of them.

- Thanks for the cigarette, by the way. I could do with that. They're hard currency in here, now I know how and why.

She then lit it and took a deep draw.

- Wow, I needed that Cortina sighed, you have no idea of the shit I'm going through. It's like all this anger is coming to the surface. You could say I've matured, like dad's finest whiskey. I suppose I don't qualify for consumption until I'm 25. Being fifteen and a bit isn't actually an asset in here. What are you in for?

- I'm saying nothing. Come on! This isn't prison! What business is it of yours? What are *you* in for?

- Losing the plot with my family, real and extended.

- Who's your consultant?

- Dr Broderick.

214

- Ah.

- He's a fucking cretin, all he does is throw out clichés. Never asks me anything or says anything constructive.

- I concur.

- Why does he do that?

- I suppose it's to level the playing field. It'd be worse if he kept throwing obscure psychological terminology at you.

- I've seen enough of that, mark my words.

- Well, whatever about Dr Broderick, he doesn't want a young person in here anymore than they have to be. We're talking weeks, not months, here, certainly not years. Believe me, I've seen it happen.

- So, it's a short-term thing, is it?

- Yes. No one is here for life anymore. We have people here who are here just because they broke up with their boyfriends. But you can't judge on surface information. There's also the problem of an underlying condition. Lord knows what is going on with this crowd. Trial and retrial, things are cyclical in there. In and out is the new being incarceration for life.

- What does he expect me to do?

215

- Just sit tight for the next few weeks. You're not going to be here forever. Those days are gone. By the way, you're a bit of a culchie, could tell by your accent.

- Shut up. You're not too far away from the country yourself.

- Suppose Freemount isn't too far away. Same as I was when I left it.

A rankled nurse burst through the front door. Her name was Carmel, and she was the head honcho. No one argued with her, however minor the situation.

- Stop trying to fix people Richareta, you're not cut out for it. That's our job. Let people buy their own cigarettes. Anyway, dinner's nearly ready.

- I'll recover when I am good and ready! There's nothing wrong with being nice to people, that makes the world go round. Life's not all bad.

- What's the story with everyone here? Not that I am in a position to judge, as you said. I'm a newbie in here, remember? I know absolutely nothing about anything or anyone, said Cortina

Richareta shook her head in dismissiveness.

- Never mind her, that nurse, Carmel, makes it her job to interfere with every conversation that happens here. Doesn't like any interaction that goes on. Like, in fairness, you have to talk to people on a daily basis, you'd go nuts otherwise!

- I definitely concur, especially if we're all in the same boat.

- Yes, she thinks she has got attitude, but just has an attitude.

- If you're not insane going in, you will be insane going out.

- Like Carl Jung said, show me a sane man and I will cure him for you.

- I'm going to boarding school once I'm finished here.

- Good luck. I hear some of those places are stricter than the prisons.

- What about meds?

- You going to ask me what I'm on?

- No. Just a lot of people are sedated in here.

- We'll, for your information, I am on just enough medication to stop me from taking over the world. Ha ha.

She remembered there and then what Hiram once said that everyone should, at least once in their lives, take a whip-round tour to a hospital ward just so you can learn how lucky they are.

CHAPTER 24

There was the predictable rattling off or hard-luck stories that was par for the course in this establishment, and Richareta had it in spades.

- There is one elderly woman, Lillian, there who came here in the 1960s aged 17 after being raped. She is totally mute unless it was to ask for a cigarette. Institutionalised, big time. Then there's Jenny. She is an anorexic girl who drove her car over a quayside two weeks back. I've seen rape victims, Ciara who self-harms, Sinead who cut off all her own hair and now wears a wig. One girl has immolation scars on her entire body – tried to kill herself several times. Her father killed her mother and has been on the run ever since and abandoned her. There's also Jill, who's in a catatonic trance after being beaten into it by her mother.

- Whatever about buying silence, you can get it for free in here. Guess I am lucky, to a point. Certainly not going down the route of suicide. Or physically harming myself in any way.

- What's this about suicide? Even if you mentioned suicidal ideation in jest? That is not funny. I'm not being funny myself, though it can be, to a point. You need a dark sense of humour in here. If you can't join them, beat them. Strange, though, nothing here is done for the thrill of it, now it is a means of survival. Seems paradoxical, doing yourself in to be free. There are a few suicides in amongst our outpatients, certainly put the Hemingways to shame. The outside is a veritable Bermuda triangle of death, in north Co Cork. So don't rush your progress.

- I suppose, as Samuel Beckett said, there's nothing quite as funny as human suffering. Whatever about me, I am my own worst enemy. Dad said as much repeatedly to me in recent days. Didn't see the joke until now.

- Now here's the real monster. There is one woman Cassandra, who is obsessed with psychics, ringing them 24/7 even though we're not allowed to have phones in here. She would steal from her mother if she had to fund her obsession. Silent illness, I think they call it. Right up there with gambling. Don't give her so much as an inch. I heard one woman gave her contract phone, and she racked up a hefty €250 bill. She only recovered €50 from her. Should have taken her to the small claims court, I know I would have.

- If she's so obsessed with psychics, don't you think that she would have spotted this coming?

- That's grounds alone for incarceration in my book. Criminal, of course. That is a serious addiction, something like a white plague. Or a silent disease? I know we are all in here due to something wrong upstairs, but this? Why not go to the AA, or whatever crowd looks after those obsessed with psychics? Perhaps even Gamblers Anonymous?

-   We'll, she's not getting my phone, for a start, it was confiscated, as with everyone's. What's her excuse? What gives her the right to use her phone 24/7 in here when the rest of us don't have them?

-   We should set up our own premium rate line, Psychotics on Line; as opposed to Psychics on Line, we'd do a better job of predicting futures than they would, if not delving into our pasts. If not a self-fulfilling prophecy, this is the loons running the asylum.

-   Would it work?

-   Don't know. Give her enough rope and she will hang herself. In addition to the phones, she bummed off other people in here.

-   Another person I should give a wide berth! Are my troubles never going to be over?!

-   Whoever made time made plenty of it. You might even have all of the eternity if you want it! But tomorrow is promised to no one! Live for today!

-   Carpe Diem, perhaps?

-   Precisely.

-   Just bide your time, sit down, read your book,

watch television now and again and let the meds do their work. You've no commitments on the outside, have you?

- Well, actually…

- Nothing that can't wait a few weeks?

- The sooner I get my phone the happier I'll be. There is someone I need to contact, between now and forever, whichever comes first.

- We're all going through phases of some description, why should you be any different? Just take it easy, you owe that to yourself. Whatever about that, there are several people in this joint who are religious to some degree, Catholics, Baptists, Jehovah's Witnesses. Could nearly set up a pan-Christian seminary in here. Bloody Americans! Have a church for every day of the year!

- Doesn't surprise me one bit. Never knew God had so many faces.

- I'm sure they will go along with the tag of poverty, chastity, and obedience.

- Funny, didn't spot any atheists there. Why not?

- I'm sure they exist. While on the subject of religion, just so I warn you, there's David in the next unit, that loopy born-again American Catholic guy. Oh no, he is coming this way.

What's he doing here? I thought he was barred from this unit.

- Who is this guy?

- Just avoid the guy, he's really freaky and has an eye for the ladies, to put it mildly. He's known as Captain Cock for a very good reason. He's been barred from visiting this women's unit as well, as I said. The Papist Rapist, they call him.

- What's he doing now coming over here if he's barred?

- If he offers you a cigarette, don't take it, it's probably laced with Rohypnol. Tell him to fuck off.

- The Roman Catholic Church is a sect anyway. So, say the Baptists, and they are legion in here.

- The hospital chaplain gets a serious doing from the people of the other denominations. They almost physically attack him while he's saying Mass, before doing some preaching of their own. He's a rock of patience, patience of a saint, of course, performing the Consecration as if nothing happened.

- And what about this guy, David?

- He's from America, if the truth be told. Apparently, he came here to avoid paying support for his kids, in that he owes millions in back payments to his wife. Got himself fired from his teaching job so he wouldn't have to pay a widow's mite towards them. Apparently to that effect he set up a symposium in the school he was working in, encouraging second level students to take drugs. They didn't take too kindly to that, so they fired him. Mission accomplished. He then adjourned to west Cork where he lived out his days.

- Does he deal drugs himself?

- I'm not sticking out long enough to find out. If he has drugs, and I know he does, they are strictly for his own personal use. Not sharing it with anyone. In that respect he's keeping his nose clean, if not keeping his cards close to his chest. You know you should never ask a druggie where they get their gear from, it's a no-no. Vow of silence, you know.

- Sounds freaky.

- I don't know why he can't pay for his kids; he had a great time making them. His last girlfriend ended up having an abortion, and then the Catholicism predictability came into play, he is pleading with her not to do it. Just as well she had the abortion, I say. He wouldn't have any means of supporting it. Even if he promised to move heaven and earth for it. Empty promises, wall-to-wall. Play the 'oh, I'll change' card. As if.

- Lesser of two evils, I should say, even if I don't

like abortion.

- He's always brags on about easy it is to shag a woman in the wards without the staff or the nurses knowing. Ditto with his gear, how he can smoke his gangya and never get spotted by the staff.

- Seems seriously oversexed to me. He's making out that he is God's gift to women.

- Captain Cock, that's his official name in here. He's not exactly drop dead gorgeous, but you get the picture. Serious charmer, you understand. Seen his type before, mark my words.

- He won't come near me, I'm too young for the likes of him.

- Oh, he's chasing after you all right, if he can get away with it. Don't see a loser as a challenge, run fast and run far. Especially the likes of him.

- Remains to be seen. Why do you hate men so much?

- I don't, it's just that I have been scalded now and again. I've reached the conclusion that if I can't be trusted to find a proper boyfriend who is in some means respectable and intelligent then I am better off staying out of the game. That and looking out for the likes of you, as I have just done now. Saved you from a fate worse than death, you understand?

- I don't need a boyfriend right now, still have to sort out the current one. No mean feat.

- Well, if you don't mind me asking, how old are you?

- Fifteen and a bit, since you ask.

- Well, in fairness, you are still a bit young for all that, boyfriends and stuff, even if you are old enough to take an interest in boys. You still haven't got your Junior Cert, have you? My mother had the right approach, that I wasn't going to start dating or going to discos until I was in transition year. Long-term, she did me a favour, even if there were a few hiccups along the way. Whatever about his looks, he's not exactly drop-dead gorgeous, but he can charm the birds out of the trees. If nothing else, he's definitely kissed the arse of the Blarney stone.

- I was told to forget Philip, my boyfriend, that was for my own benefit. That he had headed for the hills with scant regard for me. Tried ringing him, but to no avail.

- What was his game? Shag and shag off? Just get over it, dearie! Draw a line under it and move on. He's not worth your tears.

- Well, for me, it's not over until it's over, or at least till the anorexic lady sings the karaoke. I am determined to get to the bottom of this, come hell or high water.

- Well, for you, it's like experimenting with make-up when you're twelve, then it's an illicit pleasure, now it's a routine, a means of survival. Now here he comes, David, stay cool.

David approached the girls with due confidence, with a surfeit of tattoos and a myriad of gold-looking facial piercings. Not to mention the shaved head with a tuft on his forehead, not unlike the Hare Krishnas.

- Hello there little girl, what's your name?

Cortina answered him not a word. She stared into the distance, the better to avoid him.

- I asked you a question! What's your name?

Cortina remained mute. Richareta cut in.

- Look, if she doesn't want to talk, leave her alone! Get back to your unit, I'm calling security!

- What's wrong with her? Whatever about focussing on children's self-esteem nowadays, most kids and teens these days are completely full of themselves. Why are you being thick with me?

- Just leave me alone. I've enough to deal with.

- What is that fucking lesbian telling you?

- Nothing you need to worry about. I just want to

be on my own for a while, have a lot of grief to sort out. Same as everyone else.
- Anything you want to talk about? With me?

- No. Thank you. Especially with you, goodbye.

- You're very young to be in here, how old are you?

- Like I would want to tell you? Just leave me alone.

- Not to worry, I won't touch you. I'm old enough to be your dad. You can talk to me anytime, in a daughter-like fashion. I have Christ tattooed on my body.

At that he ripped off his t-shirt, to reveal a Byzantine Christ tattooed on his back.

- Okay, thanks. Goodbye. Very impressive. Please leave me alone.

- Ok, you're fine, I'll back off. No worries, goodbye.

The notice from the office informed the security that David was at it again, trespassing, for want of a better word, even if it were on hospital grounds. Carmel was once again flexing her authoritative muscle.

- David, you know perfectly well yourself you're not allowed over here. What were you doing with that poor girl anyway?

228

- Fine, I'll go.

At that, he turned on his heel and left, just in time for the Carmel to call backup security to manhandle him back to his own ward.

- Is that prick gone?

- Yes.

- Strange he asked your age, as if it was an impediment to him. If not encouragement. You know what he was up to.

- Whatever about Viagra, could there be a drug that would *suppress* sexual appetite? It would solve a lot of problems in this part of the world.

- Not many men would take it, even if it was prescribed, Viagra could be classed as a recreational drug, if you knew where to get it from. Maybe he might help the lads in his own unit. Make a roaring trade.

- I never dealt drugs before in my life, I'm not going to start now.

- Another thing about Americans, socialism is the absolute no-no. Nothing freaks them out like that. At least here we have a safety net. Communists are no longer the most threatening groups in the US anymore. I remember on the Morrison visa application form, you had to tick a box declaring whether you were a member of the Communist or

Nazi Party. Like, what are you going to say? There's nothing to stop you joining the Nazi Party or the Ku Klux Klan once you're over there, especially if you're white, Protestant and rich.

- Where does that leave him?

- He'd starve anywhere else. Socialism doesn't bother him, especially when he was showing off his brand-new Irish passport.

- You mean that this now a naturalised Irish citizen?

- More's the pity. Whatever about people giving out about refugees taking up space in this country have nothing on him. Talk about taking the piss out of the system.

CHAPTER 25

There were the sounds of screaming from the corridor. It was Jenny being manhandled by security in a very brash way.

- Poor Jenny looks like they're going to finally force-feed her this time. She's fainted in the corridor once too often for everyone's liking. Don't freak out, though. Stuff like that is pretty rare, even in here. She has a dedicated bed waiting for her in the specialist hospital in the city. God knows it's been a while since she was referred there, cutbacks and such like.

- What am I going to tell my dad? About what is going on here? About *this*?

- Don't tell him anything! First law of the jungle, don't grass. No news comes in here, nothing comes out. Check out Block C, the locked ward. You can peer through the windows there and never encounter a soul, but you can be absolutely sure that people are in there.

- You mean some disappear off the face of the earth?

- Not all of them. Most have been sedated and sectioned 24/7. For their own safety. It's like an induced coma that they're going through. For your information, try and get out of the bed by

10am. You owe it to yourself, don't get stuck in some bad habits.

-   What am I to do?

-   You don't have to do anything, just relax! No point in changing horses midstream. Don't take life too seriously, no one gets out alive anyway. I am always seeing that in young people. It doesn't happen overnight, maturity being what it is, but it should happen after a while.

-   Suppose that should cover it, all the advice I've been just given. I just want a normal life, seen enough adventure for one while.

-   Normalcy is so overrated, girl, you should revel in your lunacy, it's what makes you unique. Did you ever hear that quip: 'Reality is a delusion caused by a deficiency of alcohol'?

-   In times like these, I normally have a naggin of vodka to steady myself. Now I am on my own. Probably having withdrawal symptoms by now. Perhaps even DTs.

-   Not to mention the Smiths inspired cocktails I was so fond of becoming into the Gorbys club every week. I remember them well: I used to order a Girlfriend in a Coma, a Hand in Glove, and a This Charming Man. There was one cheeky fucker behind the bar, and he used to say to me, you have a high casualty rate among your menfolk, don't you? Trying to be smart, of course.

232

- You purchased all those for yourself?

- No, of course not! Whoever gave out about mixing your drinks never encountered cocktails in their lives. If they're not a mixture of alcohol, then what is?

- You're not an alcoholic, are you?

- God, no! Although I do know some who have been barred from every pub in town. Not giving any names, though.

- How about diabetics?

- Don't worry about them, just don't give them any sweet things, even if they get techy.

- I used to have a naggin of vodka in my inside coat pocket for social emergencies. Even if I am at the stage where I don't need it anymore. That the worst is over.

- There's detox in, and detox out. You'll know that when you have to wash all your clothes to get rid of the smell of here once you get back home.

- Thanks for the advice. I'll be that in mind.

- Anyway, all this father figure rubbish, with Captain Cock, It's all just an act.

- Whatever about father figures, I have a father

233

whom I love dearly, despite his shortcomings. He rings me twice or three times a day, it can be annoying, but I wouldn't want it any other way. It'd be worse if he didn't care, I guess. At least after this I have a home to go to, despite my shortcomings. Not languishing here till kingdom come.

A nurse popped her head around the front door.

- Cortina! Your dad's on the phone. While you are here, tell him to ring you on the payphone and not the office phone. I cannot stress that enough. What if there was an emergency? Especially if he's on your case twice, three times a day.

It didn't matter that there was no news this time, the mutual delight at the sound of each other's voice meant they could forgive them anything and they lapped up any conversation for what it was worth. Their love was reignited, and nothing, not even death could come between them now.

Once she had finished the phone call, she was back in the foyer again

- You know something, I now am genuinely sorry for putting my father through this, breaking his heart like that when he needed me the most. I know he could forgive me, but can I forgive myself?

- Well, then, forgive yourself! Your father is done and dusted, and he's still talking to you, that's something. Think it as a lesson in life and love, to quote the REM album, '*Life's Rich Pageant*'.

- Am I going to be in and out of here for the rest of my life? That's the new being incarceration for life, as someone here just said.

- Not if you look after yourself. Take the advice, take the meds, fresh air and exercise, you'll be fine.

- How long have you been in here?

- Couple of weeks, nothing too crazy, unlike me. Let's go inside.

Richareta had the luxury of a private room, as opposed to a ward. Perhaps it was just as well, Cortina having witnessed the educated mess that was the paintings, drawings, and whatever art supplies that caught themselves up in this relatively small space.

- Never mind the mess, Cortina, I'm working on something else right now.

Cortina could not help but handle the beautiful drawings, paintings and suchlike. They had more than a passing resemblance to the work of Tom of Finland, without the obvious sexual overtones, but they were still idealistic portraits of men. At that she remembered, to measure is to control, but men were doing this for centuries to women and nobody complained. She could still admire them, though, giving her a bit of a buzz.

235

- These are beautiful! I love these! You should do something about these!

- I already am. All these paintings, you see here in their own frames? These are for the various units here. Units A, B, C, D, and X.

- You donating them to the hospital?

- Donate them? *Donating them?* God knows, I sold them, of course! Can't make a living on charity or special favours, even if it is a despicable institution such as Pearses Park.

- Thought as much.

- I also have a mini exhibition in Cork Airport coming up. So, I have my fingers in a lot of pies. Can't say how many pictures I will sell, if any. Admiration just isn't enough in this world.

- We'll, in the art world, one's meat is another's poison, and vice versa. If they don't buy your pictures, don't take it personally, you have to find your niche.

- Thanks for the advice. Anyway, have to feed myself once I'm out of here, and cleaning up nicely. Anyway, I have some minor side project on the boil.

- What would that be?

- See all this coloured wool? I'm making friendship

bracelets for sale, I'm selling them for €1 each, and half the proceeds go to Amnesty international. But for you, here's one for free!
- Thanks. That's a good idea, keep your mind occupied, and boy, how you know how! And for a good cause, even better! Here's €2, to keep things sweet!

- It pays, in here, to not to be totally turned in on yourself, it's tempting, I know, but you have to start doing things for other people, inside here and out. That's the best therapy there is, and not just to get a day pass, it's the right thing to do! I hope you are taking need of which I just said, Cortina.

- I'll bear that in mind. The mind is a parachute, it will not work if it is not open.

Cortina racked her brains for possible virtuous acts she could perform, proffering cigarettes, sharing the voluminous junk food that had accumulated on her bedside table, just sitting down and talk to someone who was not Richareta, for a change. The possibilities were limited in this part of the world, but she could at least try.

CHAPTER 26

Hiram, true to form, dropped by.

- How are you? I'll ignore the cigarette but am just wondering how you are.

- As well as can be expected. How are you?

- Fine. Never mind me, what's your news?

- Well, in legal parlance, this is being bound to the peace forever. Any mischief, gone! To the Red Brick, I think they call it.

- It's not all bad. You're good to people here, so they say in here, even if you do smoke a pack of cigarettes a night. At least that's what they told your dad.

- Whatever about being a qualified solicitor, you definitely know how to lay down the law.

- All of these professions, in here or otherwise, are there to help you, Cortina. Don't forget, I have given evidence in criminal trials, I know what I am doing. I have the authority to lay down the law, much as psychologists have a right to do, with you. Let the staff here do their job, Cortina.

- At this rate you know me better than I do myself. Anyway, there's nothing strange or exciting here. How's Dad? I know he keeps ringing me, but is he ok otherwise?

- He's fine, should be discharged in a few weeks. Apparently from what I can tell, you both of you are model patients in your own fields. He needs you more than I do. And I think you have learned your lesson.

- Well, Diazepam and Xanax were once a means of recreation after a hard night's partying, now they are a means of survival. I am used to constant surveillance by now, all those doctors and nurses chasing after me, that can't be good, with meds that I can't pronounce, let alone remember, all these weird chemicals. I've a good mind to bolt.

- Don't! Please, for the love of God, don't! Not again!

- Not to worry Hiram, just testing you. Just keeping my mouth shut and my head down as you said. And not giving away more information than necessary, as you advised me. Just working my way to a day pass. Deconstructing the system from the inside.

- I don't like the sound of that, the system is here to help you, as I have said. It seems apposite that they take your phone off you while you are here. Good reason for that, so you can focus on getting better, not bother with the outside world for now.

- They could at least allow me to check my messages now and again. I haven't heard from Philip in ages. I know something is wrong.

- Ah, this famous boyfriend I've heard so much about. What's the story with him?

- I don't know. Something serious is afoot. Can't get in touch with him.

- Leave him alone if he is. Concentrate on yourself and getting better. Things will pan out, never fear.

- This is part of the reason why I am here! Lovesickness, you do the math. I am working my way to a weekend trip to see him.

- Steady on! We have stuff to do that's much more important than this boyfriend of yours. We have to sort out the house and the scrapyard, they have been falling into rack and ruin since he left. Keep earning that weekend pass, God knows we all need it, not just you.

- Okay, whatever.

CHAPTER 27

True, the day arrived when she did earn her weekend pass, but she wasn't looking forward to it.

This time, Eilís collected her.

-   You see all that stuff that's sharing the car with us?

She turned around to the back seat. She observed a heckload of cleaning fluids, brushes and cloths in the back seat, not to mention a brand-new vacuum cleaner.

-   We have to clean your place up before your dad gets back. Not to worry, though, the lads here will help you. It's going to be a hard slog, but you owe it to him.

-   I should have stayed in my bed...

-   Too bad, it has to be done. Your father is coming home soon, have to doll up the place for him.

Eilís turned the key in the lock.

Once they went inside, she encountered an awful, tornado massacre-type mess, with an overwhelming stench of mould and damp pervading throughout. It was almost palpable, and the humidity was such that with every breath she took, Cortina felt she was inhaling water, and that her lungs would be saturated by the time the job was finished. At the least it would sluice out her lungs or all the tar she had been punishing them with, with all the cigarettes she had smoked in here.

Funny, nobody thought of burgling this house. Or squat there. Was there anything here worth stealing?

- Not to worry, the insurance will sort us out. If anything is amiss, we'll find out pretty sharpish.

- How could such a mess result just from being idle?-

- Well, I've organised a builders skip, should be here any minute. The children will help you and are glad to do so, even if they had to witness the obvious *schadenfreude* demonstrated by you kindly in the course of the last few weeks.

- Well. I know where to start, intoned Cortina.

She bolted into the spare room, recently converted into a study and picked up a huge sheaf of notes.

- Good riddance to bad rubbish! This is my right to be forgotten!

- You're not taking the books as well?

- Nah, not burning those, that approach is for Nazis. Whoever would burn books would burn people and I have no intention of burning anyone.

At least not now when karma did it for me. And her laptop, that will come in handy. Am hardly going to throw that out! Just wondering what the password is, can hardly be rocket science.

She typed in the password, got it right first time.

- Password 'Ford Cortina' all one word! Bingo! Must check out the files in my own time. In this regard I will never be bored again!

- Well, there are her clothes, what about them?

- We're a similar size, so let's make use of that. A lot of those are from Gap, and Calvin Klein, so they're worth saving. Not for burning, or the charity store, come to think of it.

Cortina was taking the mammoth task in her stride, and to her unsubtle delight. It was common wisdom that if you have to do something, and that you like doing it, it carries itself. That was something worth bearing in mind throughout this massive clean-up.

- What was your opinion of Marie, Eilís?
- Psychology degree or not, she wasn't someone whom I would come to with my problems. Seemed to be a bit of a control freak, with you. However, when you absconded, she was all for leaving you to die of eventual starvation. Or the wedding kitty running out, whichever was first. Claiming your dad for herself, and herself only, talk about possessiveness. She repeatedly told him to forget you, focus on her. Sorry Solomon,

the baby gets it, she was fond of saying. That she had finished her studies with you and didn't need you anymore. You were simply excess baggage. She always said she earned her money with you and was deserving of a 1H. However, your father was never that easily convinced; he loved you and wanted you to come home. He'd have forgiven you anything for just the one time that you would come home and reconcile yourself with Marie.

- I don't understand her obsession with me. Was she hooking up with me because of Dad or did she hook up with Dad because of me? That I can never get my head around.

- Once she had her research done, she didn't seem to care.

- To measure is to control, that she did.

- But, what about the television appeal?

- It was obvious to me, she was putting on an act. You know that yourself. What was this obsession with me?

- I don't know. Erring on the side of caution, perhaps? Let's start on the rooms upstairs. Talk later, likewise gossip.

The mattresses upstairs had to go, there was an awful stench, like someone lay in there forever only to wait to die. This was especially the case with the one in dad's bedroom, the one that that was certainly christened with nefarious actions that were awful to think about. Then there was the ripping up and replacing the carpets, including her own room, which was being treated like the other rooms, with a new coat of paint, namely a warm pink, or the mushroom colour in the kitchen. As the day wore on, there was some semblance of chaos in the midst of order, as the skip gorged itself of everything related to the relatively recent past. The front garden did not escape scrutiny, being full of weeds to the last degree, solved by the planting of nice plants and shrubs.

- Whatever about the house, this garden definitely takes some beating!

- I used to work in the local garden centre, I know the difference between weeds and good plants! Unlike *some.* You do realise that you cannot plant roses where roses grew before?

- Why the hell not?

- Something like all the bugs that the previous roses are now immune to would be detrimental to the new ones.

- What about the mini-rose plant I bought for the inside? What about that?

- It'll be fine as long as you don't water it to death, as you are doing with the rest of the house plants. Mind the Busy Lizzie's!

- Where's that bark mulch? I'll finish this and get a

start on mowing the lawn. Is there any chance you could get petrol for the lawnmower, Eilís?

- Your long overdue wish is my command. I'll give you €10 for that, and the job's yours.

Whatever about industry breeding industry, it worked on time and below budget. Cortina was surprised that the whole operation was completed in their course of a single weekend, even if it was a case of many hands making light work.

- You're not supposed to set the skip on fire! screeched Eilís at her.

- Think of it as a bonfire of the vanities, burning of objects condemned by the authorities as an occasion of sin. And it's the name of a Tom Wolfe novel, better still!-

She proceeded to dance around the fire, not being naked and with no virgin to sacrifice. At least a technical virgin such as herself finally had an excuse to celebrate.

She, watching the conflagration, down on her hunkers, quietly interrogated Eilís.

- What would my mother make of this? If she had lived, perhaps.

- We'll, I do have something that might interest you.

Eilís took a photograph of Cortina's mother out of her

wallet and produced it to her. The woman in the photo having wavy dark hair, perfect teeth, nice smile. Cortina could eke out the physical similarities, but little else.

- What type of person was my mother, Eilís?

- She was named Mirinda, after an orange drink popular way back when. Horslips actually did an advertisement for that way back in the seventies. She was rather gamine, a local beauty, so to speak. She could have charmed the birds out of the trees. Very obliging, nothing was too hot or too heavy for her, always second-guessing what you were saying, she was very intelligent like that. Suppose that's where you got it from, too bright to be married to a scrap merchant. One of the last things she did before she had you was to ensure you had a university education and set aside a fund for that. She would turn in her grave to see you now, throwing your life away like that.

- Was she in trouble with me when she married? I was born seven months into the marriage.

- Yes. The marriage was rather peculiar. She couldn't wear a white dress, couldn't go up the main aisle, her father couldn't give her away, and there were no wedding photographs.

- Charming. An inauspicious start to any marriage.

- She had a bad case of what's known as post-puerperal psychosis if the truth is told. She was so screwed up she wouldn't have lasted a day out of the hospital. That's when she killed herself. Some women with PND go on to kill their babies. You were lucky that wasn't you. She was psychotic.

- But why incarcerate her?

- She would have killed everyone in her path. Your father had to incarcerate her! He was scared! You just don't want to understand!

- She would have recovered in time; he just wouldn't let her. Why didn't you just sign her out if she was okay after all that?

- Couldn't risk another pregnancy and her going loopy again. She did have supervised visits with you when your dad and you went to visit her.

- Suddenly, the supervised visits stopped. Why?

- She committed suicide. Threw herself off a high building. The same hospital, as it happened. Pearses Park, the main building. Building X, where the long-term patients are, and the geriatrics. Not much of a future for her, either way. Rock and a hard place.

- All that psychosis. It has to be hereditary. Some people should never be allowed to reproduce. Aristocrats are all inbred anyway.

- Your dad was all woman trouble, he couldn't forget you, though, like he had with everyone else. He's going to be discharged in a few days, he has to have something decent to come home to, at least something neat and tidy. He left a mess, so did you, the only proper thing is at least damage limitation.

- Never mind that, what about the scrapyard itself?

CHAPTER 28

There was a rusty gate leading to the scrapyard, with a notice engraved with a childish scrawl 'Closed until Further Notice'. The gate wasn't even properly closed, let alone padlocked. Anyone who was anyone could come and take their pick, and that meant the travellers. That was not acceptable, and if word got out, Dad was gone for sure. One's scrapyard was his castle, anything invasive was a killer.

- Well, the travellers came and helped themselves to spare parts while your father was out. Now you have to teach them a lesson.

- I'm going to sort these guys out. The scum of the earth has no business being on our property.

- You're right. Be careful, those guys fight hard when they are cornered. At the very least, those guys would steal the eye out of your head, so they will, or use a makeshift weapon of some description. I wouldn't trust them, even if I am not a racist. They know how to fight their corner, so fight hard. There's no need for CCTV, we know who these guys are, these are the Wards, doing the rounds. They're hanging around the halting sites to no good effect.

- Well, they've no right to, the fuckers. My father is not the local pushover!

- There's a shotgun and some cartridges here, if you care to use those.

- Fine. I am going to ride shotgun here till the very bitter end, if it takes me all night.

- I suppose drafting in Garda Dunne is out of the question?

- Like, yeah, right.

At the first sign of disturbance, at around 11pm, Cortina was on her guard. She took the gun and loaded the cartridges, intently looking through the window, taking aim and firing. She nearly dislocated her shoulder out in the process, if it didn't scare the travellers off.

- Get the fuck off our property! She screeched, in a high-pitched roar that would frighten the devil himself.

Eilís cut in.

- What are you doing? You'll do yourself an injury. You're supposed to tuck it into your shoulder, look! For every action there's an opposite reaction! Try it again and do better next time!

So she did. Cortina loaded two more cartridges, took a much better aim and shot, aiming not to hurt anyone, just to show who was boss. She pulled the trigger again, screeching the odds.

The boys took the hint and scarpered.

- They're gone. You don't need to do anything else, Cortina.

- Nonetheless, I am riding shotgun the whole night, just in case they come back for second helpings. Or even third helpings, as they have been doing up till now.

- You know, if you actually shot that traveller dead, you would have been treated like royalty in prison.

- One incarceration is enough for me to deal with!!

The 'office', warranted a massive clear-out, of spider webs, bracket fungus, and furthermore, of a stench of mould and damp, as was par for the course in this joint. Cortina even considered setting up a mushroom farm in there, even if she was not certain how to differentiate between ordinary mushrooms from the magic ones. Anyway, there was no one to help her on that score, at least none who would admit it in front of her. She was familiar with the mushroom policy so beloved of politicians, namely feed them bull and keep them in the dark. That was her situation.

In the course of the day, every car part you could imagine that could be dismantled, was dismantled, was catalogued, numbered and priced, out of this disemboweled mess that was the office. Every nut and bolt were accounted for, each in its own special jar. The till was computerised as well, they are having brought a brand-new computerised system to play with. Microsoft Excel never sounded so sweet, even with Eilís helping her along the way. Everything was computerised these days to the last degree, even if Dad had yet to get his head around this new technology. Everything was down to a price barcode, at the mercy of a scanner. There was a steep learning curve for Dad, but it was doable. He owed it to himself to be ahead of the latest technology.

- That's all well and good, but how are we going to get the punters in? said Eilís,

- Not to worry, I have to let people that we are open for business. Only a mint can make money without advertising, Eilís.

- What have you done, to that effect?

- I designed and printed these flyers myself! Now I have to distribute them.

She went around to cars of people going to Mass and placed flyers and adverts on their windscreen wipers, especially seeking out Ford cars, who would be the main targets.

- Special offers on various Ford parts! No job too big or too small!

The local priest, Father Hackett was aware of this, while not wishing for God's house to become a market, let it slide, because he, like anyone, was delighted to see her home, and her father on the mend, and was not averse to mentioning it during the course of his Mass during the declaration of the parish community news.

Cortina turned to Eilís again.

- I suppose we can stop short of getting a minor celebrity to ceremonially open the site.

For a second, Eilís thought she was serious. Cortina winked and she was relieved.

- You know, in some schools of thought, thinking about something is as bad as doing it.

- Perish that thought, so. This is an exercise in responsible participation, Cortina. In other words, be on your best behaviour. Got that? This is your dad's 60th birthday party coming up.

- Fine, understood. Not to rain on his parade. Got it. I know he is being discharged soon.

- Just a few refreshments and drinks and that will keep everyone sweet. Anyway, we have to collect your father, he's waiting for us. There is going to be some celebration! Him coming home, you are coming home, his resurrection of his business and his 60th birthday party! Surprise him!

- Can't tell him that. It would ruin the surprise.

- What surprise? He knows when his birthday is, and a milestone at that!

- What about the yard? Will there be enough parking space for everyone?

- If the cars spill out on to the road, too bad. Your father is a victim of his own popularity. We have to keep this as low-key as possible. This isn't the stations, you understand. Any multiple of three is a crowd. Anyway, people around here know, with military precision, when to leave.

CHAPTER 29

Regarding the party, there were cakes, alcohol, sandwiches, balloons and various sweet and savoury things, and it seemed that no expense was spared, even if it was from Hiram's pocket. Tears of joy filled Ger's eyes as he saw the rejuvenated house and grounds, not to mention having his esteemed friends and family around him, treating him like a king in his own humble abode.

- What's with the wheelchair, Ger? Are you paralyzed? Is your spine, okay?

- It's all right, my spine is fine, just crippled by recent events, emotional and physical. Not going to die anytime soon, another disaster permitting. Still not 100% out of the woods yet. Still on the painkillers, you know.

- Plugging for sympathy, no doubt, surmised Cortina. He'd be paralyzed soon enough with the drink, whatever about the wheelchair.

Never mind the recent turn of events, while Dad was the star of the show, nobody was tactless enough to interrogate *him* regarding his situation. They knew what the story was anyway, to the extent that no-one even thought of calling the Gardaí when it seemed things were about to spiral out of control.

- No good, no harm! We're happier that way!

Dad was definitely on a roll anyway, everything had fallen into place and he didn't want for anything, even if it was his birthday. He was almost drunk by now, and had a right to be, the alcohol kicking in where the painkillers left off. Even if they were over-the-counter painkillers, which was probably worse by anyone's standards.

His friends, as before, formed a tight clique, even while they were not dismantling cars right now. The knowing glances were enough hint for Cortina to vacate their personal space.

- No stirring of shit, dearie. Don't poison the atmosphere, this is your dad's birthday, intoned Hiram.

- Wouldn't dream of it. I know him better than anyone. We have an almost telepathic relationship, me and him, almost connected via Bluetooth. As if we needed Bluetooth. Anyway, he's looking for me, I think he wants something.

She gingerly sauntered towards her Dad. It was obvious he was having a good time.

- There's something to be said for saying little; if anything, the hearsay is getting a bit worse, said Dad.

- I used to believe in karma, now I don't. I don't see why you had to suffer like this, with me, declared Cortina, let nothing come between you and me ever again, Dad.

- At least here, I know where you are, and who you are.

- A watched pot never boils, Dad.

- You know how much I love you, Cortina, and I am sorry. For everything that's gone on.

- I know Dad, you've been through the wringer and I put you there, and she did too. I'm sorry as well. At least now I am up to speed.

- But I don't care about the scrapyard, I care about *you.* I've made a few calls and the Pres boarding school will have you on probation. Had to do a bit of arm-twisting to get you in there. One of those feeder schools, as they call them these days. I've got word that they are fairly strict, so be as good as gold!

- Never fear, dad.

- I would definitely say you have matured a lot in this venture of yours, that's something. I once thought that you may have been a bit spoiled, that I overcompensated after your mother dying.

- Yes, dad. And I am sorry for what I put you through.

- No amount of regret can change the past, and no amount of anxiety can change the present. I've learned that through dealing with you. I think

what the story with you and me was Rumspringa – did you ever hear about that.
- What is that?

- You know the Amish community in America? When their children are a certain age, they have a practice of letting them out in the modern world to see if they will return. Doesn't always mean that they will return. But you did. Congratulations.

- I suppose that's the law of the swallows, dad. Swallows always fly home. This summer I had all the freedom I could handle; I really needed a few ground rules. Rules aren't all bad, neither is basic cop-on.

- That is not a bad idea, Cortina. Surprised it took you so long to realise that. But experience is proved right by its actions.

- Well? Not a bad start to affairs, that's the beauty of hitting rock bottom. You can't get any lower, all you can do is start again, make a better show than you did in the first place. I might have been a little too harsh recently, but that was just me being relieved that you came home in one piece.

- Thank you for keeping me up to speed.

- You're very welcome.

- You're a late starter to the art of self-discipline. I suppose the best thing to do is become who you are. Buy the dress, dance to the music, kiss the boy, even tell your dad how much you love him, and soon! Tomorrow is promised to no one, and the past is a finite resource, live for today! Draw a line under your experience and move on. Put your experience down to experience.

- As Shakespeare said once, and I'll say it again, all's well that ends well. Comedy and tragedy in equal measure. Just have to check on you Dad, make sure you're fine.

- Oh, you're fine, no fear. Whatever about you. You were always different, Cortina, I remember when we went to the football match when you were a toddler, and you ran off with the ball! You're all the Spice Girls in one, with the emphasis on Scary.

Cortina observed the huge bonfire in the backyard, occasionally sneaking off with a sip of poitín that was doing the rounds, there was also a very large joint doing the rounds, which she chose to ignore. At that rate, she was grateful for everything in her life, even if she at one time failed to appreciate it. At this point, she was completely surrounded by love, on several levels.

- What do you make of this, Dad?

- What do you make of what?

- The poitín or the vodka?

- Not happy with that, girl, seriously. But least

you're not drinking pints. I hate to see a woman drinking pints. I don't know what it is, it's just vulgar.

- I'm not sure if this really is poitín! It tastes like battery acid.

- What are you going to do, report it to the guards? Don't drink it then. Put it in your car battery and see how far you go. That would be a legit business for that poitín distillers. That's if they are not palming it off as Lourdes holy water. Or the Johnny Jump-up.

- How do you feel about lady drivers? Do they cause most accidents, as I heard someone here say just now?

- Not at all. If that was the case, most accidents would happen outside schools and supermarkets. I have never seen this, and I hope I never see this, a woman and her kids in a three-car pile-up on the N72 at three in the early morning on a Sunday.

- What? Not even road rage? Doesn't stop some of them from charging them through the nose for the NCT. Seriously taking the piss, you understand. While you're recuperating, have you ever thought of branching out into the men's shed? Or opening the scrapyard to the men's shed enterprise?

- I've enough of my own grief to deal with. Can't be taking on any more grief besides my own. My reputation is on the line as it is. I can't build a following if I'm not there, physically at least, mending cars.

- I have sorted that out for you. Cleaned the yard and house from top to bottom, as you can see.

- You're hardly a psychopath, you do care for people. You're still a fright to God!

Cortina sidled into the living room, where Hiram was nursing a bottle of coke.

- We'll, he said, what do you make of all this? A multiple whammy, you understand? People are dying to hear your news! Not to worry, it'll all come out in the wash. People are only inquisitive because they care about you.

- And here's me thinking, Hiram, that your family had no time for me. Marie said as much.

- That's rubbish. We love you, as you perfectly well know! The kids adore you! God knows you have some stories to tell, but that'll come in time. You're just a little misguided, maladjusted, even. In a world of your own making, full of books and such like. Hard to get my head around this philosophy of yours. Or what planet you come from.

- I really was dropped on my head as a youngster. I hit my head against a stone while climbing a ditch when I was a toddler. Went through industrial supplies of Elastoplast to sort me out.

Still have the scar on my head. Look!

Eilís had to cut in.

- Well, that's something we have in common. I fell on my head as a kid and now look at me! A librarian! And what's *your* story?

- It's a story best told over a nice cold pint, mark my words.

- I've told you before, Cortina…. You're not getting any pints, or vodka, come to think of it. Certainly not pints. If you have any vodka, hand it over. That's doing you no good. Ditto the poitín. Don't think that I don't see these things. What is your story, anyway? I'm still dying to know.

- Well, in that case, I'll tell it to the kids. I can concoct a fairy tale on my situation, something that everyone could understand and say it to them. There's a lot that they wouldn't understand, so I have to word this delicately.

- Great. We'd love to hear it.

She rounded the children up in the back extension and told them her spiel, being fully aware that either Hiram or Eilís would be listening in the hallway. Talk about professional distance!

- I was exiled to a distant land by an evil witch and ended up in a strange castle. Then I travelled in this faraway land where I met a handsome prince

266

with whom I fell in love and stayed there until your father came and picked me up, because my dad was dying.

- That's fine, Cortina, but did you get married to this handsome prince? You know, the happy ever after? That's how fairy tales end. Where is he now?

- God knows, I have been trying to ring him and to no avail.

Eilís rapidly turned the corner, having intended to overhear this story.

- About this so-called wonderful guy, Cortina, play it cool! If you keep ringing him, he's bound to avoid you! If all you get is voicemail all this time, it's his way of dumping you, hate to say it. Doesn't have the *cojones* to come out and say it himself. That's typical male behaviour.

- What would you know?

- I know for a fact that women never respond to these types of hints from men, it just encourages them to keep ringing. If you're not going to take a hint, at least give him some breathing space. Just relax for a while, he'll talk when he wants to. Switch it off while you're in company, by the way, it's just basic manners. If it's important, they'll ring *you*.

At that, Cortina went back to the sitting room, dejected.

267

She alighted there just in time for Dad's speech. There was the summary tinkling of glasses, a singular music no one could argue against, even if it was something to get over with before they could resume eating and drinking, in addition to continue to happily gossip about everything that lay in their paths.

- Just to say, thank you all for coming, it's great to have you here, and for your support throughout this difficult time, particularly Marie's death. Special thanks to Hiram and Eilís for keeping everything up to speed, and the other neighbors pitching in for this particular event, making sure there was enough food to go around, to the extent that there's enough to last us until the middle of next week. But most of all, I want to commend my only offspring, Cortina, who was lost but now found, been on the tear, but now brought to heel. She still is, despite everything, the most important person in the world to me. Unlike the cars I dismantle on a daily basis, she's an unpredictable machine. Now she can do no wrong. And she's starting at Pres boarding school next semester, even better.

- Hear, hear.

- Good call, Dad, you pressed all the right buttons. Nothing recriminating or embarrassing on my part. Thanks.

- Mysteriousness can be such a pain in the ass for most people, but this is an asset for women like yourself when it comes to the opposite sex. So, if you can't be good, be careful always! Because I'll never be surprised by anything you do because you are so unpredictable.

- That remains to be seen, dad. I think you have had enough whiskey for one night.

- Well, I'm not doing it for the glory. Nobody runs a scrap yard for the glory, girl. The best I can do is just keep tipping away, excavating the coalface, one engine at a time. It's a hard slog but has to be done. That education won't pay for itself. You'd better give me my money's worth.

- I know that perfectly well, dad. I'm with you on this one.

- Glad you realised that. See? You can be good when you want to be.

- Now is the time for singalongs and even a touch of karaoke! Who's first?

Tom stepped up to the plate.

- I'm going to sing Joe Dolan's 'Good Looking Woman'.

- Funny, I always thought that Joe Dolan used to bat for the other side, so to speak. But let that not get in the way of a good singalong. Keep at it, Tom! He's hardly going to lie through song. Or karaoke, for that matter. He's probably waiting for some woman to throw her knickers at him.

Talk about finishing in style.
Then there was Pat, regaling the crowds with a delightfully off-key version of 'You Picked A Fine Time to Leave Me'.

- You know something, karaoke aside, and tone-deaf punters at that, there are groups of people who want tea, let's look after those.

Cortina ambled towards the utility room and filled up the kettles from the tap. She summarily looked over her shoulder to see if anyone else was coming to pounce on her, whether to rape her of recriminate her. There were no natural predators in sight. The entrance was pretty empty, and she was happier that way. There were, on the whole, people scouting for news, concocting various conspiracy theories as to her recent absence. That was enough pain for one day.

Dad cast his eye over the revellers, with a wistful glance over all that was going on.

- I've had enough for one night. I'm going to bed.

- Enough is right, declared Cortina. Let's get you up those stairs.

- Good. Get your priorities right from now on, said Hiram, applies to both of you.

- He's crippled, but can still manage those stairs, albeit with extreme difficulty. Cortina had to manage this single- handedly and doing this on her own was no fun. Kilimanjaro had nothing on this ascent, at least these mountaineers weren't drunk beyond all recognition.

- What happened to that bottle of Powers they gave you? You haven't drunk it all already?

- Only half it, that's enough for anyone.

- Enough is right.

- Steady on! Don't fall and crack your skull.

- A good night was had by all. Thank you for everything, Cortina, you surpassed yourself. I love you!

Once she opened the bedroom door, she aggressively flopped him down on the bed, with the minimum of sympathy.

- Sort yourself out from this on. Take off your own clothes and go. I'll put you in the recovery position, and you can do what you like after that.

At this, she walked outside and slammed the door.

CHAPTER 30

There was enough of grief in the world besides bringing it to yourself! In that regard, once the party was over, and it was well and truly over, she would almost be glad to return to Pearses Park.

Once she was back there, it was obvious to everyone that she was on the mend, being a model patient, or should that be prisoner? She realised she had much to apologize for, if not unfinished business on the outside. Convalescence being contagious, from dad to herself, the ball was now in her court.

Broderick was in his element.

- We'll, did you enjoy your party?

- Least said, soonest mended.

- Did they welcome you? Did they interrogate you? You being conspicuous by your absence all this time?

- It wasn't my party; it was my dad's 60th and this was his baby. I took a back seat and let him rip, him lapping up the attention always given to invalids. He was in a wheelchair even though his spine was fine. Talk about playing the sympathy card.

He laughed.

- All that attention seeking, has to be genetic.

- For your information, a good time was had by all. Even me.

- I'm sure you did. Ever hear the phrase 'everyone loves a winner'?

- Yes, I did.

- He definitely came out of it flying, whatever about you. You're not out of the woods yet, though yourself. You're here for the relatively short haul, though.

- He needs me!

- He needed you a long time ago when you absconded, you didn't care then, did you?

- Er…

- That's not an answer. You should have more to say for yourself than that.

- I'm supposed to give the minimum of information about myself while I'm here. I'm not spilling my guts out to you, especially if you're going to use it against me. Invading my privacy and such like.

- It's for your own good. I for one am not going to give away information to third parties.

Everything is strictly confidential.

Cortina let out a deep sigh.

- Where have I heard that before? This is not the case if it's off the record.

- In fairness, you are doing okay.

- So far, so good, so what! It's more of a countdown to extinction, this place.

- Are you a fan of Megadeth? So, is my son.

- For your information, peace sells, but who's buying? I just think that I will rust in peace.

She knew by now how to inveigle her way into getting a day pass. The squirrelling away of some refreshments for the purpose would do just fine, especially the chocolate biscuits that she purchased in the shop in Unit D, she was definitely on a winner with those. Anyway, there was only so much one could do with cigarettes, and she was keeping certain enemies closer, namely the nursing staff.

- You want a game of Switch? said Richareta, I have a brand-new deck of cards, so we're sorted! No bum deals this time, she said, suitably refreshed after her weekend.

- Great. Shuffle them, and I'll be right there with you. It's said that the most traditional games are the best of all. Plus, the fact that the library here is so woefully understocked.

-   We'll, I can hardly bring the PlayStation in here. Have to complete all the missions on Grand Theft Auto sometime. And Tekken for good measure. You can knock the living sugar out of these fuckers who are in here if you want. Not to mention that Marie, bitch you keep telling me about. Cathartic stuff, best therapy ever, video games.

Might take you up on that. What is it about computer games that they all have to be so addictive?

-   Maybe it's to do with self-fulfilling prophecy, and feeding addiction, God knows. When I was in college it was Sonic the Hedgehog or nothing. Now it's my life's purpose to complete all the missions in Grand Theft Auto. I was halfway through the missions when I ended up in here.

-   At least you have something to look forward to. What was the story there? How did you end up in here?

-   Bad marriage. Completely lost my confidence and my virginity.

-   Sounds bad. Tell more.

-   Did everything by the book. I married my best friend, he was my first love, I remained a virgin until my wedding night, cooked my husband his favourite meals, kept the house slick and span, never spoke up unless to comment on his hairstyle, and one night I came home to see all my stuff on the front doorstep, and him telling me to shift it with 48 hours' notice, that he was moving his mistress in.

- That's a bit callous. That's something that a Tory minister would do.

- I was heading here for a long time, just didn't realise it. When push comes to shove, I lost the plot. I was nasty to my friends, family and colleagues and my self-respect was in tatters, at a time when I needed them the most. Very paradoxical, you'll agree. You see why I don't get any visitors? Very few people know I'm in here, more don't even want to know, and I'm not going to tell anyone, besides this is nobody's business but my own. They would cast a cold eye on the matter, anyway. I'm not going to give them the satisfaction of seeing me like this.

- Has the divorce come through?

- I don't want to talk about that, that is my business. Thank God that the 1995 referendum was carried. Have some rights to my name. I am keeping quiet from there on in. Change subject! Scientology had nothing on him while I was with him, what with the suppression of intellect and the establishment of singular worship, centred on him, and him alone.

- There has to be someone who cares about you.

- Priced myself out of the market. If a man wants me, he'll have to swing for it.

- What about family members?

- My family members? Well, if they have no use for me, I have no use for them either. I just wish I could have used my judgement a little more wisely.

- But you did, and this happened. None of this your fault.

- Anyway, I said, fuck it, I'm living life on my own terms, I'm going to treat myself. Ergo the motorcycle. And the voluminous level of artwork that everyone has taken a look at while I'm here. You have to find out what you can do better than anyone else, in my instance, drawing and artwork, and, I must admit, I'm doing it rather well.

She indicated a large Honda affair under a grey plastic covering. Cortina resisted the temptation to sing 'Born To Be Wild'.

- That's an impressive machine. But, by the by, surely you have a next of kin?

- My brother is now my next of kin; to him, at best I am an inconvenience, at worst a pain in the ass, a blot on the landscape of the family. Anyway, as Kurt Cobain once said, 'it's better to burn out than to fade away'.

- Suppose I should count my blessings. My father rings me three times a day. Can be annoying but at least he cares. Plus, the fact that my mother's cousin comes here every other day.

- Yes, you should be grateful. My mother and stepfather have written me off, not that they cared much for me anyway. As far as he was concerned, he was not obliged to love me, that I was just part of a package. My mother couldn't get her head around the fact that my real father and I got on so well. If she couldn't have him, no one could, not even her daughter.

- Do you really hate men? Seriously? Would you know, bat for the other side?

- If I felt like batting for the other side, believe me, I would. I don't hate men anyway. You have to understand that there are seven billion people in the world, and I have been involved with a handful of them! Hardly a representative sample, you'd say.

- I suppose not, mercifully enough. Better to have a handful of true friends than a plethora of acquaintances.

- Industry breeds industry can't say fairer than that.

- Is that why you're always drawing on the go? You seem like the artist's artist, going like a train like that. It's definitely a full-time job with you, even if you are in hospital.

-   Kind of like you and youre reading and writing.
    Like Eugene Ionesco said: a writer can never take
    a holiday, he is either writing or thinking about
    writing. How about another game of Switch?

-   Great. Shuffle the cards and I will be with you.

As she shuffled the cards, Cortina was at a loss as to why
she was constantly on the go. Most people were
conspicuous by their lethargy, only surfacing in time for
their meals and the odd television programme. She was
probably bipolar, whatever that was, but she was not in a
position to over-analyse things.
Cassandra, known as Ms Psychics on Line came into the
corridor, crying.

-   Don't look now, but here she comes, looking for
    her next fix. She's just got some credit into her
    phone, so she's in her element. That's when she's
    not scragging phones off other people. Making
    out that she has no credit and wants to ring her
    mother. As if…! Making an exhibition of herself.
    Don't give her anything.

-   I won't, sure I'm more broke than she is.

-   Good girl, we have that established.

-   Do not leave valuables unattended. That goes
    without saying. Especially phones.

-   Good luck to her if she is making progress. I'm

lucky I have nothing to give her. I could very easily tell fortunes with this pack of playing cards and make a killing.

- Could you do that? perked Cortina.

- No, I'm just taking the piss. I am not gifted in that direction. How bad.

- Someone once said to me, God's greatest mercy is that he hides the future from our eyes. If I could have foreseen what I was going through now I would have folded a long time ago, but thank God, I didn't. Whatever about Ms. Psychics on Line.

CHAPTER 31

The head nurse, Carmel, accosted Cortina in the corridor after breakfast.

- You were very good this week, and you are making some progress, so we will give you your clothes and a day pass for today. How does that sound?

- Thanks. There is someone I really need to see. Where are my clothes?

- Okay. We have them here. You know the drill, be back by 5.30pm or there will be hell to pay.

Once she was given her clothes, Cortina changed into them quickly.

Richareta witnessed the whole kit and kaboodle.

- You got a day pass, congratulations! What's the occasion?

- A mission to mercy, if not mutual salvation.

- What time is the bus?

- The next ten minutes.

- Fine.

- Where are you going to?

- I'm waiting for my man! To quote Lou Reed. And I'm looking forward to it.

- Well, if they can give me the keys to my motorcycle, I will be more than happy. I remember starting a course in Dublin and the first thing they did was they took the car keys off me. Talk about enclosed orders. Would love to give you a spin home, but I only have the one crash helmet.

- Not to worry. We'll see each other on the other side, never fear. Am kind of freaked out about motorcycles anyway. Motorcycle crash victims are known in the medical profession as 'body parts', that's scary.

- Thanks for that information, as if I needed that information. You've nothing to fear from me, motorcycle or otherwise. Just as well you are going out and being left to your own devices for a few hours, those nurses are looking at us somewhat funny, don't know what their game is.

Cortina called out plaintively to the nurse, Carmel.

- Can I have my phone please, Carmel?

She gave Cortina a knowing glance, producing the prize that was the phone.

- Yes, you can have your phone, but only on condition that you make sure you come home on time. We have to check on you while you're out. That's the only reason we're giving your phone to you; once you're back it's back in storage. Got that? 5.30pm, and no later! Got it?

- Fine. Seems you are more at pains to know my whereabouts than I do.

- As I said, be back by 5.30pm, or else…! Need a tracking device with you, or even a private detective, to see how you are fixed. You don't learn everything from books, dearie. Here's your phone.

She turned on her phone, the first time in a few weeks. The incessant beeping of unread texts greeted her. She was right. Something was wrong.

It was wall-to-wall with missed calls from Philip. She rang his number, with an air of desperation and concern.

- Where were you? I tried to contact you. What happened?

- I was incarcerated in Pearse's Park all this time, where were you?

- I'm in St Jude's hospice.

- Hospice?

- Yes. It's breast cancer.

- *Breast cancer?*

- They said it wasn't necessary to have them removed, that the male hormones would take care of everything, and it was only a matter of time before I would have them gone. They are well-prepared to take them off cisgendered women like smarties, but not when I really wanted them taken out! Bastards! Suffering for my art, of course, but they can't take them out of me? Where's the fairness in that?

- That is such a cruel irony.

- Couldn't afford top surgery, Cortina, and now this. How stupid I was! I went to the hospital myself, packed my own things but now was an invalid. Just picked up a bug, I thought, I'll be fine.

- I know, but cancer? What is going on? Jesus Christ. How could that happen? How can men get breast cancer?

- Men can get breast cancer, but they have to have breasts, it comes from being seriously overweight or being born female and hit puberty as such at the right time. Please come quickly, I don't know how long I have left.

- Sit tight, I'll be there.

At that she hung up, and the bus could not come quickly enough. The hospice was an inauspicious building up a hill, having a neutral smell and holy figurines dotting every corner. It seemed unnerving that every ward was named after some obscure saint, as if to pitch a last-ditch prayer before ringing the choir invisible. The directions were simple enough, straight ahead at the stairwell, and straight into St Dympna's ward, to see Philip, in a room shared with someone who remained mute and unobtrusive the whole time. Maybe that was just as well.

- Thank God you're here!

He showered her with a million kisses.

- The transgender thing is freaking everyone out here. The other patients won't come near me. This is a women's ward, how sick is that?

- What about surgery? Maybe even chemo?

- Too late for surgery. Or chemo. Thought I'd ride out the storm. Stupid me.

- Well, binding them down tightly didn't do them any favours. How bad is it?

- It's spread. Everywhere, right down to my lungs. Lymph nodes, to boot. Game over. Whatever about abusing my body with drink and cigarettes, I'd say it was more to do with the asbestos back at the flat than everything else. Whatever about smoking causing cancer, this was a certain route to suicide, and pretty effective at that.

287

- Your voice has finally changed. That's something, even if it was too little, too late.
- Now I'm here, I don't want you to go. I don't want to die either. Don't know what's on the other side. That's why I am donating my body to science and my organs to whoever wants them. Not surrendering them to the maggots.

- That's a good thing, Philip. You go, babe.

- *Quiat amore longaeo* I am sick for love.

- Do you remember that opera we went to? 'The Nightingale and the Rose'? Do you remember that refrain? Come to my arms, we can now sing it together.

- Sing me one last song, I shall be very lonely when you are gone.

They sang the refrain repeatedly, over the course of the final minutes. They were both off-key, but that didn't matter. He quietly left this life folded in her arms and left her in tears.

CHAPTER 32

It went without saying, at least in Ireland, that it was absolutely necessary to wear something black to the funeral. Cortina was no different, having to borrow something black for the funeral, or failing that, take the whip-round tour of the local high street and charity shops for whatever was the right colour for the event. At this point in time she regretted not being a goth, or being friends with a goth, at least then she would have no problem sourcing something appropriate to wear for the event that was in it.

There was the arm-twisting with the official channels in Pearses Park to get a compassionate day pass, as long as she kept her phone on her person, and switched on at all times, however embarrassing it would be when the ceremony was going on and it would ring during the service. Not even being on silent was enough for that crowd.

Regarding the funeral arrangements, the hospice went through the proper channels, contacting the next-of-kin, namely Philip's brother. His name was Brendan. Cortina remembered Philip mentioning his name, and he hers.

- Yes, I know who you are; you're Cortina, aren't you? Philip's girlfriend? I remember he spoke very highly of you. He loved you. He said he would have killed himself if it weren't for you. I suppose he did live the life of the hermit, but that was too much in the end.

289

- What about his Facebook friends? Where are they?

- We'll, if all your friends are online, and especially through Facebook, you don't have any. But he always thought highly of you. Flesh and blood creature, so to speak, you were.

- I suppose some of the great philosophers had a female spirit guide, he was no different. Look at Boethius if you don't believe me. Or Abelard and Heloïse, don't forget. Not to mention Kierkegaard and Regina.

- Loved wisely and well, I would say, with you.

- Did you not hear? He left his body to science. And his organs to other people. Wonder how they will make of a transgendered corpse.

- I saw that. Once the service was over, the medical attendants picked up the coffin and bundled it into the van, and it brusquely sped off. Talk about standing to ceremony!

- Wasn't it strange? We were the only people at the funeral. Most funerals in Ireland take up the whole church! And then there's the professional funeral goers, sticking around for the free food.

- And the priest who was doing the service obviously wished he were somewhere else. Had to stretch himself in saying the eulogy. Didn't stay too long. He said as much that God doesn't make mistakes, that Philip had this cross to carry and was done with it.

- Come on, let's go to the local, that's enough trouble for one day.

Brendan and Cortina sauntered to the pub. It was one of those shabby-genteel establishments frequented by various male punters with little to do, except to complain about their lifetimes, and in particular, about their wives. There wasn't even the perfunctory soup and sandwiches there, as was normal for events such as these.

They adjourned to one of the snugs. Someone obviously inebriated came up to them.

- Did you finally bury the freak, Brendan? Did you bury 'it'?

- Leave us alone. We have enough crosses to carry as it is. Only God will judge him now.

- What'll you put on the headstone? 'His' name or 'her' name? Or the latest craze, 'they'?

- Just leave us alone, we've enough to deal with as it is.

At that the assailant mercifully went away. Cortina at that point really wished she could come back with witty comeback lines on the spot, even if it ultimately didn't matter.

- Well, I'm not pregnant, that's something. I'll never love the like of him again.
- He was ostracized by all and sundry, even our parents. I broke the news to them about his death, but they never got back to me. He was a lonely soul until he met you.

- You're saying he was the stereotypical deranged loner? He didn't strike me as deranged!

- Very few understood him, but you did. Living on the same floor as an alcoholic solicitor didn't help matters.

They raised a glass, the two of them.

- To Philip and his legacy! Especially having given his body to science; they will have great fun with you, brother!

- I'll second that! To the best man that ever lived. Doesn't matter what basic equipment you had; you were a true gentleman at heart.

- Never mind Philip, what about you? I can see that he's left you at a loose end. What's going to happen to you?

- Well, the powers that be gave me another day pass on compassionate grounds, on condition that I come back before 5.30pm. Will you be, okay? Being on your own with this, the local punters making unfunny jokes, if not out-and-out gibes.

- Nothing I can't handle. It's nothing compared to what Philip went through. As for you, go back to your hospital, and don't come out until you're fully sorted. God knows you've had a rough trot yourself. Whatever you do, take your time, and plenty of it. His passing means you have one less situation to worry about. Take control of your destiny, Cortina. You at least owe that to yourself.

- You mean forget Philip? How can I?

- You have no choice. He's done and dusted; the dead have no truck with the land of the living. Just move on. These feelings will dissipate over time, what are you going to do? What are you going to do, marry a corpse?

- I'll miss him and his love, she said, under a veil of tears. In some countries you can get married to someone who is dead, but I won't go that far, even if it was going the same way as the nuns. Especially when he hadn't finished transitioning yet.

- As I said, it's your life. Let the medical students play with him now. Don't hold out for a dead man, you have a lot of life to live, and a lot of love to give to someone else. You will survive, hey hey. Or *adieu.*

Cortina checked her watch. It was 4.30pm.

- I suppose each day has enough trouble of its own. I've got to head back. I have bigger fish to fry, as

293

you said. Having said that, I'll always remember him. He was my first love, and you know what they say about that.

- The best thing you can do is to forget him, forge your own path in life.

- She looked out the stained-glass window of the snug.

- If needs be, I have no destiny to forge but my own. So be it, Brendan.

They shook hands and gave the obligatory hug. At that Cortina turned out of the snug, running the gauntlet of troublemakers, and went out.

CHAPTER 33

There was the perfunctory meeting with Broderick to get over with. He was back in his element, the cast being taken off his leg and fully operational on a physical level, at least.

- Are you going to throw clichés at me again? snarled Cortina.

- Clichés are only clichés because they're true, girl.

- I have to be good at what I do to avoid stereotypes. I for one am not a cliché and will not fill into whatever bracket you put me in.

- Heard you had a bit of bad news recently. Boyfriend had cancer; I take it?

- That's none of your business.

- If it affects your mental health, it is my business.

- Never mind about him, this is about me. What's my situation? Is a diagnosis too far off?

- What do you want one of them for? I thought you didn't like clichés, as you said just now, that you were above them. Superpowered, so to speak. Anyway, if we did slap one on you would Google it once our backs were turned.

- I at least have the right to know what I am accused of. Ever hear of *habeas corpus?*

- Pride comes before a fall, you know. And you're going out with a transgender person? What does that make you?

- We fall for people, not genders. Can't say fairer than that.

- Died of breast cancer, what does that tell you. Not much of a man, was he?

- Look, I have a lot of outside interests to see to. When am I coming home? For good, that is, not a poxy day pass. I'm sick of being monitored, why do you think I bolted all that time ago? With Marie, well?

- We know that perfectly well, why do you think we have you back in night clothes? You're in a bubble of recovery, and we are not bursting it anytime soon.

- I am the captain of my own destiny. Stick that in your pipe and smoke it.

- We're talking weeks, not months, certainly not years. The days of those are gone. Sit tight and you'll be fine.

- Well, Philip dying didn't help matters. What are you going to say to that? I'm grieving on the quiet, no one can possibly know how I feel, and all because he was transgendered.

- You're right, you are in a very lonely place right now, that's where we come in, we can help you. You're not thinking straight right now. Just relax, watch the TV, chat to the other patients, smoke a few cigarettes. If you bolt now, I guarantee you that you will come back in worse shape than you were before. I've seen it happen, repeatedly. Just roll with the punches and you'll be fine.

- Whatever. Did you ever hear that song by Fester & Ailin? 'You'll Never Be Lonely In Prison!' They were right, too!

- You're not thinking straight, Cortina, being stuck in your room the whole time, crying. Sorry to hear of your loss, it didn't help matters, suffering the death of a close one, however twisted they are.

- I appreciated solitude where I could find it, for the time being.

- Well, if you are in that situation, just draw a line under it and move on. Your health is more important than any boyfriend, living or dead. Forget about him!

- Maybe you are right, and his brother said the same thing, Philip is done and dusted and dead, no point in wittering on. No one is indispensable.

- Well, I suppose that you can't timetable these

297

things, everything takes time and plenty of it! You have no deeds to do, no promises to keep, just go into the sitting room and watch television. Talk to people. Play card games for fun not money. There's always someone who's worse off than you are, if you want to talk to them. When are you happiest, in your life so far?

- When everyone is off my case.

- It would be worse if people didn't care, Cortina. Think about that.

- Strange, I bolted because I was just attention seeking, now I have all the attention I could possibly hope for. Talk about being a legend in my own lunchtime. What's the deal?

- Well, you're definitely matured during your stay, and you have something on the outside to look forward to, besides the recent agony. I'm going to discharge you on licence. How does that sound?

- You mean you're letting me go?

- On licence, of course. Any trouble and you're back in here sharpish!

- Not to worry, Broderick, I won't be in here again, never fear.

- The less I see of you the happier I'll be. Get out of my sight, Cortina.

- Great. Just get my things together, and I'll ring my dad.

- Not so fast, we'll ring your dad for you, we have to give you a prescription first, this could take a while. And yes, we will be ringing him on the office landline and not from the payphone!! And while we're at it, not from *your* phone!

At that, Cortina careered towards the ward, industrially sorting out the detritus and rubbish on her bedside table that accumulated in the time she had been here. There were various soft drinks, and boxes of chocolates and Pringles to beat the band. It was too much for one person to ingest, whoever wanted a healthy lifestyle, and she was all too ready to give these items away, Richareta shook the bedside curtain that encircled the bed, to let Cortina know she was there.

- Are you ok? Are you decent?

- Pretty much, given the circumstances.

- You were with Dr Broderick. What's the story with you?

- Discharged on licence. My dad's collecting me in a few hours.

Richareta was downcast.

- Well, I'm happy for you that you're better, but I am going to be lonely. I will treat you to a game of Grand Theft Auto, as I have promised, once we're out. Perhaps order a pizza, and some fries. Not to mention a few cans, keep it sweet.

- God knows that there were more movements in this place than in the Macarena.

- Here is ironically, here where you're safe. Its real life that gets you every time. Don't come out halfway, you'll regret it big time. I know you don't like Dr Broderick, but you can't say fairer than that.

- There are a few things for me to do once I come out, I hate being at a loose end. There are a few wrongs that needed to be righted. But I'll never forget you.

- Vice versa. You are the truest, most sincere person I have ever met.

- And that ex-husband of yours, well, he didn't know what he was throwing away. It's his loss. Remember that. Here's a large bottle of coke for your troubles.

The next port of call was Jenny, still weakened despite the effects of the force-feeding.

- Jenny! I have something for you!

- What do you want?

- I have a large bottle of orange for you. Don't worry, I haven't opened it, thought you might have it. It's not the diet stuff, my apologies, but it'll see you through.

- Suppose it would be churlish to refuse.

- It will last you until next month, mark my words. Thanks. Now please leave me alone.

The next port of call was Ciara, being unusually bubbly and animated for someone who was in here. Not to mention someone who made a habit of cutting herself.

- I suppose you heard about that guy Matt Talbot, who wrapped himself up in chains?

- I'm pretty much ahead of him, with the self-mortification business.

- Why do you do this to yourself?

- Feel I deserve it, if not for religious reasons. Self-flagellation down to a tee.

- I don't know. There is enough suffering in the world besides deliberately visiting it in on yourself. I don't understand self- inflicted pain, not the physical kind, anyway. Here's some chocolates, and a bottle of lemonade. Take a break from the mortification for a while. Not even Matt Talbot was at himself 24/7. His corpse would have thanked him for it.

- Wow. Thanks. No chance of a few cigarettes, while you're standing?

- The cigarettes are mine, by the way. No one's touching those, even if they are hard currency.

- Actually, I think your dad's here.

Dad came in his new, second-hand, red Ford Mondeo. There was a surprising amount of junk accumulated during her stay that nevertheless managed to be stacked in its entirety in the boot of the car. There was too much that could be palmed off to others, so she stuffed them into ready-and-waiting cardboard boxes Dad brought her and went on her way. Funny, though, what seemed to be a hours-long job only lasted around 30 minutes! Including packing the stereo.

Richareta knew a song befitting the occasion.

- In can see her unloading boxes in my mind. That's from Hüsker Dü, the song is 'She's a Woman, and Now He is a Man'. It's from the *Warehouse: Songs and Stories* album. Thought you might like it. It's worth checking out.

- Good, Richareta. Am more of a *Candy Apple Grey* person myself.

- Cortina! When you're ready!

- I have all my stuff here, let's go!

- Is that it? he said.

- Pretty much, Dad.

Cortina and Dad got into the car together, simultaneously fastening their seatbelts.

- Dad, have never seen you so perky. Whateve magic bullets they are giving to you now, keep taking them!

- You're all the magic bullets I need, Cortina. Let's go!

- Now, let's have some music! What'll it be? Horslips?

- Horslips' first album, *Happy to Meet, Sorry to Part.*

The first thing on arriving back at the house, was to wash her clothes to get rid of the stench that was the hospital of Pearses Park. That was no mean feat. The stench of cigarettes was ever more pronounced, due to having too much time on your hands, except to smoke your brains out. At least the washing machine and dryer were in perfect working order, whether or not would stay that way after this gargantuan load was anyone's guess.

CHAPTER 34

Whatever about tying up loose ends, the old school was one place to start. She went up the avenue with the DVD player tucked in under her arm. As luck would have it, the school was open, ahead of the Leaving Cert students getting their results sometime that week.

She approached the principal's office with due caution. The secretary, Vonnie was there, but Cortina wished to speak to the organ grinder, not the monkey, even if it was Sr Eucharia.

- Is Sr Eucharia around?

- Yes, she's here. What do *you* want?

Her timing was impeccable, Sr. Eucharia having promptly arrived with a large cup of coffee in her hand. Once she saw Cortina, it was obvious that she was stunned.

- Well, to whom do we owe the pleasure, Cortina, hmm?

- Thought you might want this. I don't need it. I repent. I am sorry.

- What's this about returning a DVD player? We all knew you didn't need it; it was just a technicality before you got expelled. Why return it now? Your expulsion is a *fait accompli*, we can't take you back. It would just look bad on our part we have to take a hard line with miscreants like you. Sorry if you were just an example of us to take a hard line with discipline, and another statistic at that.

- Whoever said anything about coming back? I had tie up some loose ends. I'm not the proverbial prodigal daughter. I'm not sorry. I'm just offloading unnecessary baggage and I will be on my way. You need this more than I do. As you said, it makes no difference to my situation with you. Never apologize and never explain, it's a sign of weakness.

- Can't fathom as to why this is such a tower of strength, or of character.

- We'll, it's like Elvis Costello's solo albums, you know, those which he did without the Attractions, *Spike* and *Mighty Like A Rose*. They weren't well received but he loved them all the same. Even his fans said so.

- Elvis Costello sings about stuff you wouldn't understand, no, seriously.

- Not to worry, they're still great songs.

- So what? That doesn't explain your situation sufficiently for me to feel sorry for you. We'll, it's a shame about Ms. Masterson, dying so suddenly.

- Yes. That's unfortunate. She did have it coming.

306

You can't cheat karma, you understand.

- What about your father? What wrong did he do to anyone to suffer all this?

- That's what you get for encroaching on the relationship between a rebellious teenage girl and her dad. That is criminal. Like a grizzly bear and her cub. Whatever about bears, I for one am not going to hug Marie to death.

- Good to hear that your education did not come to an abrupt end, Pres, I heard, are taking you on. They're fairly strict, knock off a few sharp edges off you.

- I suppose just keep my mouth shut and my head down and apply myself for once.

Eucharia smiled.

- Good to see that you are finally on the right track. Goodbye, she said, and good luck.

She did not neglect to ask if all this was all going to be broadcast over the whole school, even if it wasn't during term time.

- It wouldn't be the first time that this has happened, eh?

- I have now realised that energy cannot be created or destroyed but can be converted into another form if needs be. See? That's something that I

307

learned in school.

- Well, if you can convert negative energy to positive energy, I would be more than happy. Everything's in your hands, Cortina. Use it wisely. Seems like we don't have to perform an exorcism on you after all. All for the sake of being popular.

- It was never in my mind to be popular, just sincere. I suppose the reason I was the class clown was that I was clinically depressed underneath it all, now it's caught up with me. You ultimately have to deal with these things head-on, or they bite you in the ass, like it did with me.

- I suppose if you can't believe in karma, at least believe in fate. You can be everything you want to be, even if it is just being yourself.

- Yes, sister. Indeed.

- As they say, if you don't change your path, you'll end up where you're headed. Goodbye and good luck.

Eucharia sidled back into her office, as if nothing had happened, or anything said. That was almost insulting how quickly the conversation began and ended. There, however, was no blame on either side, there were divergent paths between them and they both had to be forged, barring the mutual forgiveness clause.

Then, there was the phenomenon of the Cigarette tree.

Cortina, like everyone, needed a stiff drink and a cigarette after getting their results. She looked over her shoulder, and saw Andrew O'Connor coming out the front entrance.

- Hey there, Andrew! What's the story?

- Just got my results. Turns out that I got Law!

- Congratulations. Your hard work paid off.

- Yes. You are coming out later?

- Not really in the mood for socialising. My dad is still on the mend. He needs me, in the few weeks before I go to Pres. I could commute to Bruce College, but that's a bit awkward. Pres is where I'm headed, as a boarder, more's the pity.

- Good luck then.

- Precisely. I'll need it, son.

- Is it true that they open your personal mail and read it? Ditto email and Facebook? Censor everything going in and out?

- I'm bracing myself for that.

- Anyway, what happened with you? There was a tip-off that you adjourned to the Glanmire woods to go and cut your own throat. There's a lot of Satanist and hard-core Christian fundamentalism going on down there, it depends on who you listen to. Kinda weird, since you don't swing in either direction, even though they had to check it out.

- It did cross my mind to go into some quiet corner and slit my throat. But life is what happens when we make other plans.

- To paraphrase Jim Morrison and The Doors, you broke on through to the other side.

- They don't make rock stars like they used to, including me. I don't want to throw everything away. Everything's precious, I'm precious as well, at least now. I'm not suicidal, if ever I was. I have my good and bad days, but never suicidal. I'm not depressed. Even if I was stuck in Pearses Park for the last while.

- Never mind that. You have vodka and the ciggies?

- I have some here. I am one of the dying breeds who doesn't know how to roll cigarettes, so here they are, ready-made. Draw the line on vaping, though, doesn't have the same ring to it.

- I know that psycho teacher died.

- Yes. Even if they did marry, they'd have been divorced within the year. Put my last euro on it.

- 'Waiting for the Sun'. That's The Doors again. You made it in one piece and came out of it flying!

- You and me both! Forging our own respective paths in the universe.

- Like George Orwell said, war is not meant to be won, but continuous.

- I don't know what they are going to make of you. You know, Pres.

- Never underestimate the power of an underestimated woman, Andrew. If you're going through hell, keep going, so said Winston Churchill.

- That's you down to a tee. Always on hand with your apt quotes, and one-liners.

- Whatever about quotes, there's someone in this town whom I really should see. Goodbye, and best of luck with Law!

She left Andrew and made her way to the Three in One. Kryztyn was behind the counter, reading a newspaper. It was quiet at the moment, with a slow trickle of students getting their results, and he had plenty of time to kill.

There was the tinkering of a stereotypical wind chimes upon entering. Kryztyn was above delighted to see her.

- Cortina! Good to see you! Where have you been?

- Here, there, and everywhere. What's your

excuse? You still here?

- Still here. Tipping away, as you would say in Ireland.

- Telling tales out of school, simultaneously feeding my brain with the best books on offer. I just spotted a new Polish grocery shop just down the road on my way here. What's the story there? There's a veritable Polish quarter cropping up here, you're right at home.

- At least I'm not lonely, as I was when you went missing. The crowd from the mart kept me on my toes. Anyway, what would you like?

- Flat white and a chicken wrap, as usual.

- Good. Sit down there and I will bring it down to you.

- How's things under the three-year lease?

- Things were a bit iffy at first, but things picked up eventually. It definitely got to be the place to be seen among the students from the various secondary schools, to the point that I had to extend the café out the back. It paid off, mark my words.

- You had no choice. You were stuck on a three-year lease, had to make a go of this place.

- God knows, there's only so many crystal rosary

beads one can sell! The primary school students are killers for that, but not much more. 'Made to pray with, not to play with'.

- That's where the smart money is, teenagers. Have the highest disposable income of any socioeconomic bracket. Remember White's, on Black's Street? That used to be an old man's pub, I know because I went in there as a nipper with my dad. It even had that old pub smell. Now it is known as the White Horse, and it is seen by the young crowd as the place to be. You should check it out sometime.

- Not really a fan of the trendy pub circuit. Just a quiet pint does it for me.

- What about the lonely farmers on a Friday afternoon? Are they still there?

- They're still there, never fear. Have to be here due to the latest drink-driving laws. They didn't see that as worth their while going to the pub, just hob-nob with their friends here, go to the off-licence pick up a few cans and go home.

- Doesn't sound like much fun. You sink your drinks and that's it.

- Plus, the fact that the gardaí are out on force on the main road every Friday afternoon and evening with the breathalysers. A farmer can't take chances in his job, especially when he has to bring shedloads of silage bales back to his sheds.

Or drive his tractor around the farm and locality every day of his life. What good is a farmer without his driving licence, let me tell you?

- Suppose you can't blame yourself if they get done for drink-driving.

Those naughty boys, have no sympathy for them. Even if I have to listen to them wittering on about the prices, they make on selling their cattle. God knows I have seen it. Anyway, you're a culchie yourself, you do the math

CHAPTER 35

The months trundled through and Ger consoled himself with the various vehicles that were gone past repair. He buried his loneliness into taking apart some miscreant vehicle, dodging the obvious questions that his friends asked while he was on this duty. In any case, he had to weather the storm of solitude that constantly hit him hard when he ached his way to sleep. Every solitary night. At length, he resisted the temptation to ring her constantly; he knew he had to cut her a bit of slack. A surveilled pot never boils, anyway.

It was at this point that he threw himself on the tender mercies of what was known as the Men's Shed. He opened his doors to anyone with an underlying mental health condition to have some purpose in their lives. It was good to talk, take his mind off things, and as time progressed his own agony dissolved away through the phenomenon of association. Whatever being ruined by praise, these guys definitely earned their money! He was at a loss to ascertain whether he got more out of it than they did.

As is said, the proof of the pudding is in the eating. There arrived, in the hard-and-fast month of April, a letter from Sr Magdalene Cusack, Principal teacher at Pres. on top of Cortina's report card. He was not looking forward to this, but he had to bite this particular bullet.

Dear Mr Murray,

I am writing to inform you about your daughter's academic progress in this school. There were a few teething problems to begin with, but she has since settled in well. She is what be classed as a model student. Cortina has since demonstrated herself to be a determined, organised and committed student, and has worked very hard so far this year. Most people mature as they get older, and Cortina has it in spades. She is a joy to teach, and eager to learn! I can safely say that up to this, that the system has failed her. She needed a bit of discipline, and plenty of it. But now it's fine. Pulling her weight, so to speak. Leaving certificate won't know what hit them! I hope that she continues her studies here and should she care to do so, she would find herself a very welcome student here.

Yours sincerely.
Sr Magdalena Cusack
Principal, Pres.

These missives came home in time for the Easter break. Cortina and Dad began to appreciate each other's company now, even if scandalous news was fairly thin on the ground. There was the decree of *omerta* that pervaded the atmosphere when it came to what went on in school, even when you were in the comfort of your own home.

- Well, there is your sixteenth birthday, and that fact that you did so well in school. It coincides with the Easter break. An event worthy of celebration! I've made a few calls, so you don't have to do anything. Just go down to the corner shop and get some sweets and minerals. Plus, there is €50 for you to get a haircut and make-up.

- Good call, Dad.

- So, you're finally a woman. In every sense of the word. Matured a lot, from what I gather.

- Americans make so much of this particular milestone, the sixteenth birthday, even if you have to wait until you're 21 to drink. They even throw parties when you start menstruating. So what? Periods are literally a pain in the ass. Messy and inconvenient at best. And for what? Preparing every month for some creature who hijacks your body for nine months, and everything else thereon in, for the rest of your life.

- Don't say that Cortina, a baby is the best gift you can ever receive, even if it's a death sentence at your age.

Kryztyn supplied the catering, free of charge. He said with all conviction that this was in in recognition of loyal service, even if Cortina was out of the loop for some time. This is a 'thank you' for supporting him at the outset, when things were slow to take off and he was really terrified he wouldn't last the distance.

- I know that it's early bird-type stuff, but what the heck? He really is a great friend.

Cortina looked stunning in her little black dress, with her

317

hastily bought jewellery and hair style, along with her make-up that she was still at pains to apply right. This get-up was a welcome reprieve from the stricture of Pres.

Hiram and Eilís, unsurprisingly, were there, enough to see Cortina fill up a glass of orange. Unadulterated, of course.

- You on pledge, Cortina? You ran out of vodka?

- Pretty much. Had to sign a Pioneer declaration before I even got past the front gate. As if I would get into trouble there! Eschewing cigarettes and alcohol for the rest of my life. Or at least until past leaving certificate.

- Whatever about impossible dreams were, they are now accessible. Now you have your whole life ahead of you! To die unfulfilled is the greatest tragedy of all, Eilís declared.

Hiram cut in.

- Your success is nothing short of aerodynamic, if not meteoric. Just don't let up just yet, there's no room for complacency. Even if we did have to suspend our disbelief on the outset, you're doing well.

Dad could not contain himself.

- You're looking very well, sweetie. Never seen you as immaculately made up as you are now. You're all grown up now! Physically, at least.

318

- Well, you always get to where you want to go.

- Talk about metamorphosis! Are you still the same girl who we used to know, who rejoiced in making life hell for everyone? The bane of teachers everywhere? That head teacher at Pres is mad about you! Keep up the good work girl!! He shouted, making it obvious that everyone was listening.

He took Cortina aside. He opened a small box and produced a princess-cut diamond necklace.

- This is a princess-cut diamond, because you are my princess. And a diamond.

- I'm hardly a princess, dad! I'm not precious about anything! Just roll with the punches. By the way, thanks, dad. It's beautiful! Though I can't wear it to school; they're very strict on wearing jewellery in there. Not even pearl studs goes past them. But thanks anyway dad.

- You're still my princess. You are the most precious thing in the world to me. I love you Cortina. You're priceless, almost like this necklace.

There was the determined, aggressive buzz that was a hardcore-looking motorcycle. Once the helmet was yanked off, she could see it was Richareta.

- Oh my God! It's you, Richareta! Great you could

come!

- I wouldn't miss your birthday for a Led Zeppelin tribute concert!

- You came out of it flying, Captain. You're looking so well!

She gave her the warmest of hugs.

- Got you a small gift, said Richareta, reaching into her backpack.

She produced a medium-sized parcel. Cortina readily opened it. It was an immaculately bound handmade journal.

- Something to keep your mind occupied when you're not studying. Even the studious likes of you need a break. Of course, you need to have a creative outlet! Poetry, stories, you name it. Everything goes in here, even if the teachers want to take a look at it. They won't be bored! Even nudge you the way through publication. You won't be bored either, mark my words.

- That's ace, Richareta! Couldn't ask for a better present.

- Well, it's something to keep your occupied between games of Switch, or Grand Theft Auto, or even Tekken. You still haven't taken me up on that yet, you know, on school breaks and suchlike of computer games. Remember how you wanted to knock the sugar out of all those people who made your life a misery? Hey, now's your chance, however virtually realistic. Show those fuckers who's boss.

- As you know, I've been busy. Once the summer comes, we'll definitely do that!

- Your wish is definitely my command!

- Great to see you again. What you have been up to?

- Tipping away, doing paintings, such like. Have an exhibition in the library in Charleville pretty soon.

- Just send me an email with some photos and that will do, under the circumstances. Did you sell any paintings while you were in Carrigaline last time I was talking to you?

- A couple here and there. Not ideal, but it's the luck of the draw. As you said, one's meat is another's poison, those paintings I sold to Pearses Park kept me sweet for a while. Not to mention the show in Newmarket. That was pretty good, by all accounts. As I said, I have an exhibition in the library in Charleville pretty soon. I know you'll be back in school by then, and they have a stranglehold on you there, but I am sure you'll be there in spirit.

- No word on Captain Cock?

-   No, I haven't seen him recently, and I'm happier that way. Ploughing through the female population of the locality, whatever nefarious magic he's working on them. Good luck with it, that's all I can say.

Eilís popped her head around the door.

-   Cortina? A guy called Andrew is here to see you.

-   Bring him in! Would love to hear how Law is treating him now! Hello Andrew! How are things?

-   Just tipping away, girl. You have to work hard in this business, but that's no problem for you from what I gather. Looking forward to seeing you there next year. The Cigarette Tree is not the same without you.

-   I'm sure it will get along fine without me. There will always be someone who will take up the slack. There will always be someone who will think it's cool to smoke, even if it is anything but. Glad I kicked the habit when I did.

-   Speaking of smoking, congratulations on kicking the habit, Cortina.

-   I had no choice. In there it was cold turkey or nothing, after three weeks I had it made, though.

-   And what about the vodka? Where's that gone to?

- Don't be so idiotic! Of course, you can't have drink in there! I'm on pledge while I am there, whether I was inside or out. The nuns in there would nearly breathalyse you on your way back in!

- Do they strip-search you? Like Category A prisoners?

- Not going that far. Despite what you may have heard, it's not completely like prison. Even if they do read your incoming mail and emails, if you're not careful, the system will drive you nuts. Just keep your mouth shut and your head down, that's the only actual rule in that place.

- Point taken.

Eilís tinkled her glass.

- Speech! Speech!

Cortina alighted the makeshift platform in the front yard. She was all for hobnobbing with individual punters, and not exhibiting herself, but in fairness, this was her party, and she would cry if she wanted to, even if the occasion did not demand it.

- Thank you Eilís. I don't have a speech prepared, so please bear with me. Just to say, thank you all for coming to my sixteenth birthday party, I'm delighted to have you here. First go-off, credit where credit is due, namely Dad, who has moved heaven and earth to make sure I had the best education possible. For being patient through my tearaway days, and for keeping the memory of my mother alive. For my absent mother, I know that she is looking down on me from above and from the good friends and neighbours who have seen us through all is, you know who you are. I suppose I should mention for singular mention Hiram and Eilís, and Richareta, who came by specially by motorcycle from Freemount to be here. To all our past and present friends, not to mention those we will meet in our future endeavours! There's still plenty of food, and plenty of drink, so sport yourselves while you may!

Eilís, once the clapping was over, came over to Cortina, with obvious intent.

- Good call, girl. Couldn't put it better myself. Nothing incriminating, towards anyone. I was on the lookout for that. Maybe some reference to Marie.

- When you put it quite so bluntly, yes. I wasn't going to mention Marie, why would I, at an event like today? Look at everyone, eating, drinking, probably giving in marriage, even if it is an interesting prelude to Armageddon. I'm happy the way things planned out, even in the knowledge that tomorrow is promised to no one. Look at everyone here. Who's going to be around this time next year? You? Me? Anyone?

- Well, on the other hand, who will be born this time next year? Who's up the duff already, or who knows if they are? Life is like playing relays. When you've finished your course, you pass the baton on to someone else.

- Good way of putting it.

- I will tell you a true story. In the local Arts theatre, there were two women working there for the summer, one training to be a midwife, and another an undertaker. I had to laugh, I said to them, whatever else, between the two of you will never be out of a job.

- What will happen to us in the meantime?

- Suppose have fun, I guess.

- In that regard, I'd better set up the karaoke machine. There is no greater satisfaction than seeing Dad's friends massacre the classics with delightfully off-key versions of the various hits. I suppose listening to that and all our sins will be forgiven, what do you say? Come up here, Hiram! I know you have it in you.

- Steady on, Hiram's never drunk enough for that. Just as well.

- Neither am I. But it's fun to watch, even if it is a one-off basis and he can't sing.

- How about you then? The occasion demands it.

- Maybe in a while. Have to sink a few drinks for that to happen.

- It's not a competition, Eilís, step up to the plate.-

- There's are two types of people in world, those who are willing to sing, and those who are willing to let them. Guess where I fall in.

- I've never seen such an ebullient crowd here, ever. Everyone is having a great time; haven't seen it like this in ages. I haven't had this much fun in ages.

- Whatever about your speech, unrehearsed as it, what would you wish for to all those people in here who have come here to see you, and to see you in your glory?

- Well, Eilís, my one wish is that the doors would open, and they would all walk out.

And, for a split second, Eilís thought she was serious.

TABLE OF CONTENTS